TANGLED PAST

BARNETT SPRINGS ROMANCE

LEAH BRAEMEL

Somerlane Publishing

TANGLED PAST

A shot-gun wedding to a stranger wasn't Sarah McLeod's first choice to escape her abusive stepfather but her new husband Jackson Kellar's calm dignity gives her hope that she might finally achieve the happiness she's sought all her life. Until she realizes that Jackson has already given his heart to another man.

Even as ranch hand Jackson Kellar's love for his new bride deepens he cannot shake his desire for his best friend and ranch owner Nate Campbell. Nate thought he'd found the perfect wife, one who has the spirit and grit to survive life on the Texas frontier. A twist of fate has left him standing helplessly aside as Sarah slowly falls in love with his best friend and lover.

After Sarah and Jackson are offered an opportunity at independence away from Nate's ranch, they're faced with a difficult choice—one that will give Sarah a respectable life but destroy the two men's relationship forever or accept Nate's more scandalous solution and face a judgmental society's censure.

PRAISE FOR LEAH BRAEMEL

...a sweet, believable ménage story with the perfect balance of plot, emotion, and steamy sex.

— FRESH FICTION

...a story that will take the reader on an emotional roller coaster...

— BOOK BINGE

5 Stars and a Top Pick: Once again Ms Braemel has made her story come to life and taken me along on the journey

— NIGHT OWL ROMANCE

A Barnett Springs Romance

Also by Leah Braemel

Barnett Springs Romances

Texas Tangle

Tangled Past

Feeding the Flames

Texas Hook-Up

The Grady Legacy

Slow Ride Home

No Accounting for Cowboys

Wrangling the Past

Hauberk Protection Series

Private Property

Personal Protection

Deliberate Deceptions

Perfect Proposal

Hidden Heat

Stand Alone Stories

All I Need for Christmas

Unashamed

DEDICATION

To my family, for listening to me endlessly talk about my characters and for offering up advice— sometimes sage, sometimes hilarious.
Thanks also to Tabatha S for everything she's done, including kicking my butt when I needed it.

CHAPTER I

"Danged devil's rope." Jackson Kellar checked the stallion's withers where the barbed wire had nicked it. "It ain't too bad though, Nate. Shouldn't be a problem for the trip back home, less it festers."

"Good. McLeod was right about this fellow being high-spirited. It should be a treat to ride him." Nate ran a hand down the horse's neck and crooned softly until it gentled. Nate had mighty talented hands when it came to soothing the beasts. Or any other animals he came across.

Jackson included himself on that list.

Aware of the McLeod field hands watching them, Jackson positioned himself between the horse and the hands to check his six-shooter. Something about the look of some of those men left him uneasy. Once assured the gun was loaded, he surveyed the ranch. Long strands of the barbed wire outlined the fields and pastures, where a decade before this valley had been open. Not that it stopped the cattle rustlers from tearing down the silver barriers. Rumors he'd heard in town questioned just which side of the McLeod fence the rustled cattle were herded.

A flash of pale blue hurtling at Nate had Jackson whirling on his heel. He cocked and aimed the Colt until he realized Nate's attacker was a shovel-wielding woman.

He holstered his weapon and watched the she-devil swing the shovel at Nate with an admirable ferocity. From the way he was deflecting the blows instead of landing his own, Nate must have figured out she was of the female persuasion. If the woman was as pretty from the front as she was from the back, Jackson couldn't blame him.

"Need some help there, Nate?"

"Nope, I got it." A grinning Nate dodged the shovel, and again when it returned for a yet another go-round. She'd put so much oomph into it, she lost her balance. Seizing the opportunity, Nate snatched the shovel and tossed it to Jackson, who caught it one-handed.

Danged if the she-devil didn't ball her hand into a fist and catch Nate with a right hook that snapped his head back.

"You sure you don't want some help?"

"Naw, I got it." Nate caught the fist as it whizzed past his face a second time, pulling the hellion against him. "Now, see, ain't this more cozy, darlin'?"

"I'm not your darlin'." She jammed her knee into a part of Nate's anatomy that no knee had a right being anywhere near.

The color drained from Nate's face, and he dropped to the ground with a croaking sound that had Jackson wincing in sympathy.

With a growl, Jackson caught Nate's attacker from behind. He banded his arms around her, trapping her arms at her side.

It didn't stop her from hauling her foot back to continue the assault.

"Your mama know you use language like that?" Jackson asked, keeping an eye on Nate, who was turning a disturbing shade of green.

"My mama died last spring." She stilled, her voice dropping to a whisper.

"Well now, I'm right sorry about that. But you can't just go around attacking folks for no reason."

"No reason?" The hellcat started struggling again. "You're on my family's land, stealing my horse. If I'd had my gun handy, I could have shot you and no one would have stopped me."

Her family's land? So this was Josiah McLeod's chit? The one Nathaniel had in mind to propose to? This was the woman who might take his best friend, his lover, from him?

Her parentage explained why the ranch hands weren't lending a hand to the fight. They weren't about to interfere with the boss's daughter. Or if the stories they'd heard about Josiah McLeod were true, the hands were quite happy to let the girl get into trouble so they'd have a front row seat at her punishment. He gentled his tone. "Now haul in your horns for a second. We weren't stealin' this here horse. Nate bought him fair and square."

Still on his hands and knees, Nate shook his head like a dog that had just crawled out of a pond. "You can check with your pa if you don't believe me. Ask him about me—my name's Nate Campbell."

No reaction to the name. So her father hadn't mentioned they were here for more than just the purchase of the horse. Well, wasn't that just dandy. "As I said, Nate here bought Bandit and a couple of mares from your pa." And had talked about offering Sarah his hand. Something both her father and Jackson thought was unusual considering Nate had never met Sarah before. "Deal was done fair and square."

All the piss and vinegar she'd had before disappeared. "He really sold Bandit?"

Jackson took a chance and released her, but he didn't relax his guard, staying ready to grab her again just in case she decided to take another shot at Nate.

"Yes, ma'am. Your pa never mentioned this was your horse though." He found that omission interesting though there may have been a financial reason that the daughter hadn't been made aware of.

The bay in question watched them as he paced the fence line on the other side of the pasture.

"Bandit, and a couple of mares?" Sarah's eyes narrowed.

Right pretty eyes she had too. Dark like coal over high cheekbones, with full lips that a man could lose himself in for a week. Lips that would look mighty fine tight around a man's cock.

In her struggles, her bonnet had fallen to the ground, and strands of long black hair feathered along a strong jaw. Pity she'd pulled her hair back into that god-awful bun, but it probably was easier to care for that way rather than letting it get tangled up in the wind when she was riding.

"Yes, ma'am. I'm guessing he never mentioned Nate's name? Never told you to expect him to arrive today?"

Her lips thinned. "Mr. McLeod doesn't discuss business with me, so although he told me we'd have company today, I had no idea you'd be taking my horse."

Her blue calico skirts highlighted a nicely rounded behind when she bent over and picked up the shovel he'd dropped on the ground. Out the corner of his eye he saw

Nate flinch, but Sarah simply hefted it and headed back toward the house.

"You all right?" he asked when Nate staggered to stand beside him.

"Yup. She caught me unawares is all." Nate adjusted himself with a grimace, but he didn't take his eyes from watching Sarah's behind swing as her long legs ate up the dirt between them and the family home. Like her horse, she had a strong and wild air, so different from some of the frail young misses coming west these days.

"She's something, ain't she?"

Nate's sighed comment had Jackson's head turning toward him. Considering the way his own cock had reacted to her, he couldn't fault Nate's taste.

"I find it interesting her pa sold her horse without tellin' her in advance." Censure filled Nate's voice.

Indignation for her, or a memory of his own father doing the same thing to him when he'd been a lad?

"Or that I was considering offering to marry her." The ice in Nate's voice could have frosted the ground for a dozen feet around them.

"Maybe McLeod didn't think you were serious considering you'd never actually met her. Or maybe he deliberately didn't mention us, or the sale of her horse, because he knew she'd react this way and would scare us off."

"You're thinking that rumor we heard about what McLeod was plannin' for her is true?"

Jackson rocked on his heels as he considered the question. And the indignation in that question too. Looked like Nate was smitten and might offer for the girl's hand as they'd discussed on the trip over.

Ah, well, he knew it was too good to last. Besides, it was

probably better if Nate did take a wife. Their relationship was downright dangerous. A woman in the house would put any rumors to rest. Of course, he'd have to find somewhere else to live if Nate wedded.

"Do you think he's still planning to raffle her off?" Nate prompted again.

That rumour had been the reason for this trip. Nate had written the letter to Josiah McLeod, both for the sale of the horse as well as the offer for Sarah's hand, the evening after he'd heard the rumour. It was just like Nate to rescue a woman he'd never met before.

Jackson shrugged. "Can't rightly say until we actually meet the man and can take his measure."

"Guess we better follow her then." Nate dusted himself off.

Jackson bent down and picked up Nate's hat and held it out for his friend, admiring the bruise starting to form on Nate's jaw. "She's got a good right cross, I'll give her that. Wonder if she'll have a similar spirit in the bedroom?"

Color tinged Nate's cheeks. "Come on, let's get this done."

They caught up to Sarah just as she reached the barnyard, where her father was talking with two men, the younger one bearing such a striking resemblance to him he could only be McLeod's son. Though Josiah's hair was red and younger man's hair white blond, there was no mistaking the protruding family chin and freckled complexion, so different from Sarah's jet black hair and golden skin.

Looked like the rumors about Josiah's wife bedding someone other than her husband were true.

Who the third man was, Jackson had no clue. Middled forties, whipcord thin, sun-dried skin. Hard look in his eyes. Ranch hand, he guessed at first from the lariat the man carried, but revised his estimation when he drew closer and noticed the expensive tooling on his chaps and fancy silver belt buckle. Neighbor, perhaps? Another buyer of one of the horses? Or for Sarah's hand?

Both McLeods frowned at Sarah's approach, while the third man openly leered.

She positioned herself in front of her father so Walt was between her and the third man. "Did you sell Bandit?"

For some reason he couldn't explain, it annoyed Jackson to no end that neither of her kin seemed to be bothered by the other man's lecherous expression.

"Yup, sure did." Josiah McLeod's frown deepened, especially once he caught sight of Jackson and Nate leaning on the fence, watching.

"Mama raised him and trained him, and gave him to me. He's mine."

"Listen here, girl, that horse is *mine*. Just like everything else on this land is mine. Including all those animals who are eatin' my feed and filling stalls that I could fill with animals that'll pull their weight more than you or that damned horse. So don't you go getting all high and mighty because I sold a half dozen of my own stock without seekin' your approval."

"But they—"

"I ain't sayin' another word on the subject, girl. You live here on my good graces, so don't push your luck if you know what's good for you. Now you go get dinner ready." McLeod tilted his head Jackson and Nate's way. "We've got two extra guests, as well as Jed sitting down at the table tonight. You make sure the grub's good, ya hear?" He headed to the barn, leaving her staring at him, her shoulders slumped in defeat.

As Walt sauntered past, he spit onto the ground in front of Sarah's feet so it splattered across the tips of her boots and muttered, "Lazy squaw."

Jed strolled up to her and whispered something so low Jackson couldn't hear, but whatever it was, Sarah's eyes widened and she took a step back. He was about to jump over the fence to intervene when in front of his eyes, the hellcat regained her confidence. Two seconds later, Jed was curled in a ball on the ground, gasping for breath and clutching his balls as Sarah stalked into the house.

"Damn, she's somethin', ain't she?" Nate breathed, admiration filling his voice. Guess Nate had either forgotten his own experience with Sarah's knee, or he'd decided it was admirable when used on someone else.

Still moaning, Jed hauled himself to his knees, then his feet. "Fuckin' squaw needs a good beatin' to teach her her place." He spat in the direction of the house. "If I was McLeod, I'da dropped both her and her ma off at the nearest whore house as soon as I'd realized my wife had fucked a goddamned Indian. If I'd let 'em live in the first place."

With a pointed look at Jackson, he resettled his hat and headed for the side of the house, where a flashy thoroughbred had been tethered.

Jackson grabbed Nate before he vaulted the split rail and went after the stranger. "Don't. He ain't worth it."

"Someone should set him straight, stand up to him." Nate shrugged him off. "How come you aren't going after him?"

"You mean considerin' I've got Indian blood in me?" Jackson shook his head. "He wouldn't learn nothing from it. Besides I'd probably end up with a bullet in my back or a rope around my neck for attackin' him. As I said, he ain't worth it."

"She's worth it." Jackson almost missed Nate's whispered, "So are you."

CHAPTER 2

Sarah crawled into bed and pulled up the quilt her mother had made for her tenth birthday. It was one of the few things she had left of Mama's. That, and a turquoise beaded hat band, that her momma, right before she died, had whispered to her had originally belonged to her real father. Thank heavens she had found a place to hide it so neither Josiah or Walt could take it.

She sighed and turned on her side. Bit by bit, Josiah had been getting rid of anything that reminded him of his wife. Her mother's body wasn't even cold when he'd informed her she must refer to him as Mr. McLeod, not as Pa. Strangely enough she'd been relieved at not having to keep the pretense. She'd managed to save some of her mother's dresses to remake for herself, but almost everything else had been purged from the house over the past six months. By the end of the week, Mama's prized horses would all be gone. Bandit and three of the mares to Mr. Campbell, the rest to various ranchers in the valley. She hadn't missed that none of the others—Walt's paint or her stepfather's cutting horses—were for sale.

How long before he got rid of her too?

A glass clinked downstairs followed by a creak. Josiah or Walt —or them both—getting into the whisky, no doubt, and settling into their chairs for a long drinking session. She rolled her shoulder to ease the ache, though whether it was from the hours of ironing she'd done earlier or scrubbing the floors, she couldn't tell.

Smoke from their cigars drifted up through the cracks in the floorboards. Josiah said something, but the words didn't carry. Another voice murmured a response, something about the horses that had her paying closer attention. One of the men who had arrived today—Jackson—had been relegated to sleep in the barn. His...boss? friend? had been offered a bed in the bunkhouse. Maybe he'd come back to discuss something with Josiah? The sale of her horse, along with a half dozen others, had already been finalized over dinner.

Or had Jed Hasley come back?

Her skin crawled as she remembered his suggestion out in the yard. At least Josiah hadn't punished her for kneeing Jed, despite Walt's argument.

"We can make it work. You know we've done it before and not had a problem." From the clarity of his voice, Walt must have been sitting at the table directly beneath her. "With me and Jed and a couple other guys I can round up, we can take the two of 'em easy."

Two what? Or was it two who? Damn it, she couldn't hear what the others were saying. Taking care not to tread on the boards that she knew would squeak and give her away, Sarah crept to the head of the stairs. She settled in the shadows at the top in time to hear Josiah speak.

"You'd have to make sure that damned stallion can't be traced back to you once it's done. And make sure you get a good price for him. Bandit's got a good blood line and is worth every penny he can bring."

Sarah covered her mouth with her hand. They were going to steal Bandit from Mr. Campbell and resell him?

"Not a problem, Mr. McLeod." Damn, it was Jed downstairs. Hopefully Josiah wouldn't let him come upstairs again. "I can change the brand up easy enough. By the time I'm done with it, no one will be able to connect it with you."

Change a brand? How many times had they done this before?

"All right, but you be careful when you approach them." Josiah paused. She imagined him swilling his drink or perhaps refilling it already. "That Campbell fellow shouldn't be a problem, but the other one may be trouble. Make sure they can't recognize you, and if they do, make sure they can't tell anyone about it."

"We'll kill him and his friend, save any problems in the long run." She could almost hear the smile of anticipation in Jed's voice "What do we do with the squaw? Do we take her too and sell her off to someone in town?"

Squaw? Walt meant her. Had they sold her to Campbell and his friend like she was horseflesh too?

"I don't care what happens to her. Fuck her as many times as you want, then sell her off to the whore house like we originally planned. Just cover your tracks so no one who might come looking' for Campbell will end up here."

A floorboard creaked as someone walked across the floor in her direction. She scrambled back to her bed, her heart pounding so hard she was certain they'd hear it all the way downstairs.

Someone had to warn Mr. Campbell and his friend they

were going to be attacked. Before they left. Maybe if they left earlier or took a different route, they could avoid the attack.

Once the back door closed, and Walt and Josiah had both retired for the night, Sarah rolled from beneath the covers. She crept down the stairs, careful to keep to the side where the wood planks wouldn't creak as much, and avoided the third stair from the bottom that creaked no matter where she stepped on it. After a moment's indecision, she decided to go out the front door—it didn't squeak on its hinges the way the one in the kitchen did. She paused by the coat rack and grabbed her cloak, then fumbled in the dark to find her boots and tug them on.

The half moon hung low on the horizon, leaving the yard in shadows that hid her as she picked her way across the rocky ground. She stopped when she spotted a figure leaving the bunkhouse, a quick step but glancing around almost furtively as if he didn't want to be seen. She kept to the shadow of the spreading oak in the middle of the yard, watching as he approached the barn. He stopped by the door to the tack room, once again surveyed the yard again before tapping on the door. In that last glance around, before the barn door creaked opened and he disappeared inside, she caught a glimpse of the face beneath the hat. Nate Campbell.

Why was he acting so furtive? Were he and his hand planning on stealing the horses in the middle of the night, to leave without paying? Or were they planning on stealing more than what they'd come for?

Or was Mr. Campbell just seeking to talk with his ranch hand, discuss the plans for their trip home? She owed it to them to find out which.

To her relief they'd left the door slightly ajar and she could slip in without the darned door squeaking, announcing her arrival. Once she was inside the barn, she had to rely on the few slivers of moonlight breaking through the gaps in the barn boards to light the way. She stopped when she heard a low murmur in one of the corners.

"Stop squirming." Amusement tinged Jackson's voice. Was Jackson his first name or his last? He'd not been invited to dinner, or even in the house, so they'd not been introduced. "You're gonna end up with salve on everything."

Salve? Had she hurt him worse than she'd thought? Would he take it out on her once he got her away from the ranch. That's what Walt or Josiah would have done.

"I can't help it. It's cold." There was a pause. "I sure wish you'd let me go after that Jed fella. I woulda liked to have seen him eating my boot leather. What he said about her wasn't right. He shouldn't have been allowed to go unchallenged."

"I know, but he's the type to pull out a knife and stab you in the back. Might have even poisoned your food. I've seen that type of man before and you wouldn't have stood a chance. Hells afire, I bet that younger McLeod would have joined in, held you for Hasley."

She stifled a sigh. Walt had never batted an eye when someone insulted her. In fact he usually joined in with sharply honed insults that he'd know would hurt her. Yet here were a stranger ready to defend her even after she'd attacked them. What would it be like to be part of a family who supported you like that all the time?

"Still wasn't right," Nate grumbled.

Straw rustled, one of them switching positions probably. Sarah was about to step forward and announce her presence when Jackson spoke again.

"You're really going through with this, aren't you?"

"Yes. I am."

Going through with what?

"What if you don't suit? What if she's not happy or she refuses your proposal?"

"I suspect she'll be happy enough to get away from McLeod and his son. After that, I plan on doing what I can to make her happy."

Wait? They were going to take her with them? Had Josiah sold her as he had the horses? But as what? A maid? A mistress? Surely this 'proposal' wasn't for marriage. Who married someone they'd never even seen until that day?

"What if you're not happy?" Jackson's voice was quiet.

"It doesn't matter. I need a wife, Jack. I need children to pass the farm onto. I need…"

"Someone to divert attention from us?"

A long pause. "Yes. That too."

There was long pause before Nate spoke again. "Don't be jealous of her, Jack. You know I love you. I will always love you, but we have to be realistic. You know it's for the best."

"Doesn't mean I have to like it." More straw rustling, followed by Jackson again. "You fancy her, don't you, Nate?"

"Yes, I do. She's pretty. All that hair black as crows' feathers, and those big brown eyes of hers." Nate chuckled lightly. "Besides, what's not to love about a gal who packs a mean punch to protect her horses? She's got a fire about her that I admire."

Merciful heavens, most men, and some women, found her hair and her Indian traits disgusting. Yet this man liked that about her? If she hadn't already liked him, his comment sealed the deal. At least until she remembered no one was giving her a choice.

Jackson's laughter was more of a deep rumble, like thunder in the distance. "Or a mean shovel."

He just had to bring that up, didn't he? She must have looked like a wild-eyed hellion. Especially when they'd bought Bandit fair and square.

There was a moan and a sigh, following by more rustling hay.

"You know this will have to be our last time. We can't do this after tomorrow. I wouldn't expect any woman to accept..." Nate's voice lowered and no matter how much she strained to hear the rest she couldn't.

Whatever they were doing, she felt like she was interrupting something personal. Something private. She briefly considered returning in the morning to warn them but that might be too late.

Even when she did tell them of Walt's plans, would they believe her? What if they didn't? If she told them now, what if they did and went charging in to confront Josiah and Walt?

"You want to warm your hands? That particular part of my anatomy ain't fond of ice, thank you," Jackson said.

They weren't sleeping, but what they were doing, she had no idea. She gnawed on her thumbnail, only half paying attention to their words.

"Sorry. Guess I ain't warmed up from washing yet. The water was danged cold."

Just where were they apply salve that it took both of them?

There was long, heart-felt sigh. One of them, Sarah couldn't tell which, made a hmming noise, then the barn fell silent again.

You have to tell them at least to be careful. Or to take a different route home. If Jed does ambush them, ambush *us*, because she figured she would be given no option but to accompany them, Jed planned to rape her, to dump in a whore house. And they'd be dead.

Sarah took one step forward, only to stop when Nate spoke again. "Sarah sure can cook, can't she? Not that you'd know it from the way Walt ate. She might as well have poured his portion in the danged pig trough the way he slurped it up."

"Yup. Talking of eating...I got something you can eat." Jackson chuckled, a pleasant sound that warmed Sarah's chest in a most peculiar way. It was chilly out, but not enough to make her nipples harden beneath her cloak.

Curious as to what they were talking about, she crept forward until she could peer into the stall. While most of the stall was in shadows, thin wedges of moonlight sliced through several holes in the walls high above, illuminating where the two men lay. They'd pulled their bedrolls together. Supporting himself on one elbow, a shirtless Nate faced Jackson.

Parts of her body she'd never been aware of before pulsed deep inside her as she watched Nate undo Jackson's shirt buttons. He spread the fabric wide, revealing a hard chest and flat stomach. His fingers played with one of the dark pebbled nipples, flicking it between his thumb and forefinger.

Oh! Oh my. She pressed her hands to her mouth and took a step back. Josiah had lately taken to quoting passages from the bible to denounce her mother's adultery. Some of the passages had mentioned men touching men, talked about such behavior deserving death. Without thinking she leaned closer, unable to look away. How could such tenderness be a sin?

Would a man do that to a woman too? Under the cover of her cloak, her own hand mimicked Nate's, tugging and playing with the hard bud of her breast. Her knees weakened, and she leaned against the stall wall. Oh dear heavens, what would it feel like if a man touched her there instead of her doing it to herself?

Nate's hand disappeared beneath the cover. Jackson

moaned, hips arching up and hands fisting at his side. "Oh, fuck, Nate, I'm not going to last long if you keep that up."

The cover fell away, revealing Nate's hand encircling Jackson's erection. He pumped up and down along the shaft, his thumb moving over the bulbous head. Dear God, she'd never seen anything so scandalous. So beautiful.

Sarah didn't think she'd moved or made a sound, but Jackson jumped up from the bedroll and stared at her as if she'd shot a pistol. She whirled and raced for the door. He grabbed her before she could get out of the barn.

"How long have you been here? What did you see?" His words cracked through the air like a whip.

She opened her mouth but didn't know what to say. For a woman, she was tall, but he topped her by half a foot. A sliver of moonlight slanted across his face, accentuating the sharp planes of his cheekbones while hiding his eyes in shadows. The light also highlighted his lack of clothes, the broad expanse of chest, and flat belly, a body finely honed by hard work. Her gaze lowered, drawn to his still-rampant arousal. It suddenly occurred to her how stupid she'd been, walking into the barn, alone with two men who could do whatever they wanted to her with no one to stop them.

"Damn it, what did you see?" He shook her, not so it hurt, but hard enough that her cloak fell to the ground.

"Nothing. I swear." She closed her eyes, reminding herself that it wasn't her he lusted after, but another man.

Footsteps crunched outside. He released her as he ducked his head around the barn door. His expression was grim when he returned; he grabbed her forearm and dragged her into the stall, swinging the door shut with his foot.

"Stay quiet," he commanded in a furious whisper, yet she instinctively knew the fury wasn't directed at her. He was angry that she'd caught them, true, but more likely he was angry at himself, she realized, possibly even afraid she'd denounce them.

Light. Whoever was coming must be carrying a lantern. They'd find her. Here. In a stall with Jackson. Who was most decidedly naked though his arousal had softened. It wouldn't matter that she was still untouched by a man when they found them together. Josiah had been looking for a way to get rid of her, and here she'd handed him the means on a platter. She could tell the McLeods that these men weren't interested in her but knowing her father's sense of justice, these men would end up strung up by their necks, and she'd still be abandoned at a brothel as a soiled dove.

"I saw her go into the barn, I swear Pa." Walt's voice floated through the crisp night air.

She cast about, searching for somewhere to hide.

"Ha! Here's her cloak!" Triumph filled Walt's voice. "See? I told you Jed was telling the truth about her sneaking into the barn."

Jackson cursed under his breath; he shoved her into the darkest corner and trapped her against the wall. She shrank into the corner and made herself as small as possible. Despite her efforts to make no trouble, was she about to find herself abandoned, forced to work as a streetwalker to earn her next meal?

The stall door swung open and her father stood there, lantern in hand. "I know Sarah's with you, Kellar. I can see her nightdress behind you."

After a moment's hesitation, Jackson stepped aside.

Josiah's eyes narrowed, his expression cold and assessing. "Walt, fetch the preacher. Now."

CHAPTER 3

Preacher? Hellfire! Jackson cursed, both fate and Sarah. Though it would have been worse if one of the men had walked in on them without Sarah being here. They'd both known it was too dangerous to be fooling around when there was a possibility someone would walk in on them. Out on the trail with only the cows and horses for company or in the privacy of Nate's home, they could let their guard down but not here. They deserved to get caught for being so danged rash. But now Sarah was going to be caught in their tangle of lies.

"Your boss may have wanted to marry this whore but you've saved him some trouble now, haven't you, boy? Now he'll have two hands to work for him instead of having to present a squaw as his wife. Like deserves like, I always say."

A strangled sound came from the corner of the stall. McLeod swung the lantern in that direction, his eyes boggling when he spied Nate standing there. "You were with the two of them at the same time?"

McLeod swung a meaty fist in Sarah's direction, but

Jackson deflected it into the wall before it connected. From behind them, he heard the sound of a pistol cocking.

"You want to hit someone, you can hit me or Jackson," Nate growled. "Not Sarah."

"She's mine to discipline, not yours."

Discipline. Yeah, he had a good idea of the type of discipline Sarah had already endured from McLeod. From her half-brother too.

Jackson shook his head. "If you're gonna force her to marry me, then she's mine now."

McLeod's lip curled. "She ain't yours until the preacher says she is."

Sarah rubbed her arms where he'd held her. Damn it, had he hurt her? "Nothing happened with these gentlemen, Mr. McLeod. I came out to say good-bye to Bandit, that's all. Nothing happened, I swear."

Nothing she'd better talk about, or else he and Nate might find themselves swinging from the barn's rafters right soon.

Josiah's glare turned from Sarah to Jackson and raked downward. Thank God his erection had flagged as soon as he'd spied her. "Nothing happened? I find you in your nightdress in the same stall with one man who's buck nekkid and another man with only his britches waitin' his turn, and you think I'm going to believe nothing happened? You're getting married as soon as the preacher gets here. Then I can finally wash my hands of you." Glaring at Sarah, he pointed out of the stall. "Get your bee-hind in the house and get dressed. Now."

Sarah ducked as she slipped past him, as if she expected to be cuffed. Or worse. But McLeod didn't move until after she'd darted out the barn door. Then he shouted, "And start packin', 'cause you ain't spending another night under my roof."

"Proves she's her mother's daughter down to the bone,

don't it?" Jed leaned a shoulder against the stall door behind Josiah. "Ready to spread her legs for whatever man comes sniffing around."

"I'll do right by her, McLeod, but Sarah told the truth." Jackson held up a hand to stop the older man from speaking. "Nothing happened between us. I give you my word. I'll be taking her virginity in our marriage bed."

"You're lucky I don't shoot you both and bury your bodies where they'd never be found." McLeod's lip curled in a sneer.

"If Jed here hadn't seen her come out here on her own," Josiah continued, "I mighta thought you two had kidnapped her without payin' me. There's not a judge in the land who'd convict me."

Why had Jed been watching the barn? Or was he watching Sarah? Perhaps Sarah was lucky they'd been here too, or Jed may have used the opportunity to force himself on her. If he hadn't been the reason she'd slipped out to the barn in the first place. Once again he thanked whatever fates had intervened so the male McLeods hadn't been the ones to discover him and Nate together.

"You don't have to marry her, Jackson. I will," Nate said quietly.

Jackson glanced at Nate. It really was the answer. Nate had a house, not to mention his land. Three thousand acres would support a good-sized family. And McLeod was also right. Given the way society judged a person by the whiteness of their skin, Sarah would be looked down upon by most of Nate's friends as being unworthy of him. But Nate really had seem taken with the girl. Would he look upon their marriage as betrayal of their friendship?

"I'll marry Sarah," Nate repeated. "Just like I planned."

McLeod raised one eyebrow and considered Nate for a

moment, then shook his head. Pointing to Jackson with the rifle, he said, "I found her with him, not you, and he's the one who's naked as a jaybird. You at least still had your trousers on. I'd not ask a man to raise another man's brat like I had to. 'Sides, I expect Sarah and Kellar here will suit each other better."

Since they're both half-breeds—Jackson heard the implied insult.

McLeod took a deep breath and focused on Jackson. "I expect you to take her off my land as soon as the preacher's done hearing your vows. I don't want that girl back here again. She's been an embarrassment to me long enough."

"You can count it." Oh, yes, he'd be putting as much distance between him and the McLeod ranch as he could, and as fast as if his britches were on fire. Of course he'd be accompanied—not only by Nate but by a wife of all things.

Jackson maintained his guard until McLeod was out of sight, then he snatched up his trousers with a curse.

A hand on his forearm stopped him. He looked up to see Nate more serious than he'd ever been since he'd known him. "I meant it, Jack, I'll marry her. I know you..." He glanced away. Even in the dim light the splash of color rising in his cheeks was plain to see. "I know you don't want to get hitched to a woman."

His fingers curled into a fist out of reflex. "You know I've been with women before. What the hell did you think me and Lavilda Taylor were doin' the nights I stayed over at her place?"

"I just..." Nate looked away, his nostrils flaring. "I thought maybe it was a show. To fool people."

Now if that weren't the pot calling the kettle black. He couldn't stop his irritation from venting. "Is that the reason you courted Eliza Owens last fall?" He lowered his voice to a hiss. "To prove to yourself you could still get off without my dick up your ass?"

It was a low blow and he knew it, so he didn't bother blocking Nate's punch. Or the next. The third one he deflected. As he'd expected, Nate's whole body followed the swing. He stepped in and caught his friend in a headlock, then whispered in his ear, "I ain't any different from you, Nate. It don't matter to me if it's a woman or man I'm with. Same as you."

Nate sagged against him. "I figured…"

"You've been telling yourself that you were with me because I made the first move that first time, haven't you? That you weren't the pervert in this relationship, that you were under my power or somethin'? Because it wasn't your idea?"

"No." There was no conviction in his tone.

"We both know you'd been watching me for months before I finally approached you."

Nate twisted from his grasp so Jackson let him go. "I know what I did. What I am." He walked to the barn door and stared at the house, its yellow kerosene lamplight deceptively warm and cheerful against the dark November sky.

Was he wishing he'd been the one caught with her?

Forced to marry her in the morning? Or did Nate doubt Jackson would be a good husband, considering what they'd been doing? Yeah, he'd been wondering that himself.

NATE STARED ACROSS THE SHADOWS OF THE YARD. Would McLeod be going after Sarah, beating her for sneaking out to the barn? He sure as shooting had been angry. Would

Sarah tell McLeod what they'd been doing? He had no doubt she'd seen enough to get them strung up.

The drapes in the downstairs of the house hadn't been drawn. With the kerosene lantern still lit, Nate watched McLeod pour himself a whisky in the kitchen. He was more troubled that there was no sign of Walt or his buddy Jed. A shadow fell across the curtains on one of the upstairs windows, a silhouette of a feminine form, her bodice pulled tight as she reached for something. The image disappeared as she snuffed the light, the window a black rectangle in the dormer.

Would she try to get out of the marriage by telling McLeod what she'd seen?

Images of Sarah decrying them, of the McLeods and their farmhands turning on them, raced through his mind. The skin on his neck prickled as he imagined the noose being placed around it. His arms and legs twitched at the thought of being forced to straddle a horse or stand on a box, while the rope was flung over a tree branch or barn rafter. Of the rope snapping when whatever held him up was kicked from under him. Of the noose tightening, strangling him.

He'd seen the bodies left hanging by lynch mobs with vultures and crows picking at the eyes of the corpses, been sickened by the stench of flesh rotting from the bones in the damned Texas heat.

How the holy hell could they explain it so they wouldn't end up swinging from the rafters come morning?

"I'll try to be a good husband to her, if that's what you're worryin' about." Jackson had come to stand beside him and stared up at the window too.

He met Jackson's gaze for a moment before slowly nodding. "I know you will."

"We both knew it would end up like this."

Bet you figured it would be me who'd get hitched first. Ma would have been pleased to see him settling down, even if it was to a woman with Indian blood. Until her dying breath, Ma hadn't given up her quest to find a woman who would keep him in line and give her grandbabies. She would have defended Sarah at church against the women who would whisper the sordid details of her mother's indiscretions. Maybe Miss Martha would stand in her stead.

"If I could change McLeod's mind, I would." Jackson sighed. "You'd be better for her, no question about it. I ain't got nothing to offer a woman 'cept for my hat, my saddle and my horse."

It took all of Nate's strength not to touch him right now, but he had a feeling if he did they'd both shatter. He rubbed the back of his neck instead in a futile attempt to ease the impending headache he knew would soon hit. "You and Sarah will do fine. You'll...do fine."

And so would he, despite how the world felt as if it was spinning out of control. After all, outwardly nothing had changed. He and Jackson could still work together. Still be friends. Only part of their *relationship* would have to end after tomorrow. A part neither of them should have had in the first place. Maybe this was God's way of keeping them on the straight and narrow.

Jackson shrugged on his shirt. "Look, since I ain't got a place of my own, would you let us live in that cabin you got out in the back of your place? Just until I can find us another place to live? A woman deserves her own bedroom and her own kitchen. Somewhere she can fix up and call home."

Nate snapped shut his jaw after it had dropped. "That place is one step shy of bein' a woodpile."

"I can fix it up."

"The roof leaks like a sieve. The chinking needs to be replaced, unless you want Sarah to die of pneumonia. The privy stinks to high heaven no matter what way the wind is blowin', not to mention the bats and all the other critters who are livin' in it. Even the hands prefer to sleep outside instead of using it when they're checkin' the lines."

Jackson swore under his breath. "You're right. She'd take one look at that place and turn tail. What the hell am I going to do?"

Wasn't it obvious?

"Why don't you bring her back to my place?" He waved his hand in impatience when Jackson looked as if he was going to argue. "My place has more than enough room for us all, and it's nicer than that old shack."

He gathered himself and lightly squeezed Jackson's shoulder. "She's gonna be skittish for a while, Jack." She isn't going to be the only one. "This is the only home she's ever known, and we can both tell she hasn't had anyone in her corner her whole life. At my place, she'll have Miss Martha to help her out or talk to whenever she needs a woman's advice, or to introduce her to the ladies in the church." Cut off any gossip they might dish. "She deserves better than what she's had here."

She did. In so many ways. So did Jackson. But it was going to be awkward, the three of them living together. Painful for him watching Jackson and Sarah go to bed, knowing what would be going on between them.

Jackson paced the length of the barn. At any other time he would have made some smart-mouthed comment about the way his friend's backside flexed, or the play of the lantern light on his shoulders, but Nate knew better than to say anything while Jackson worked it out in his head.

Eventually Jackson returned to the doorway and stared at the McLeod home again. "You're right, Miss Sarah probably misses her ma. I hadn't even thought of that. Having a woman close by might be the best thing for her."

"It would."

"Still, I'll need to work on building our own place. It ain't right that we impose on you forever."

Nate swallowed at the thought of being apart from Jackson. In the meantime, this might be his last chance to show him how much he'd miss him. "How long do you figure it'll take for the preacher to get here?"

Jackson stared into the night sky, his brows drawn together. "It's a good ninety minutes' ride into town, and then McLeod'll have to find the preacher, convince him to come out in the middle of the night instead of waiting for morning. Ninety minutes or more for the trip back, dependin' on if the preacher rides horseback or uses a buckboard. So five hours, give or take an hour, I reckon. Why?"

"Do you think anyone would have a reason to come out here any time soon?"

Jackson shook his head slowly. "I doubt it. Why?"

Nate shut the barn door and jammed a bar through the two handles so no one could open it easily without them hearing. "'Cause I want to give you a proper good-bye."

He reached up and cupped Jackson's head, drawing him down until their mouths met. Jackson tasted of burnt coffee, but he couldn't have tasted better to Nate. They clung to each other, their tongues tangling, their hips grinding against each other before Jackson broke off the kiss.

"I can't do this, Nate. It's too dangerous. And it ain't fair to Miss Sarah."

CHAPTER 4

"It's not a death sentence, darlin'," Jackson murmured.

Sarah jerked her head up. His dark eyes assessed her, not in judgment but concern. "What?"

Clean-shaven and in the soft glow of the oil lamps lighting the lounge, Jackson didn't look near as scary as he had last night. Especially when he pressed her knuckles against his lips with a fleeting kiss similar to the way he'd kissed her in front of the preacher that morning. He leaned forward and lowered his voice so the folks in the hotel lounge wouldn't hear. "Bein' married to me ain't a death sentence."

No? So why did *'til death do you part* still pound in her ears louder than Bandit's hoof beats on a hardpacked road?

Sarah swallowed as he lifted her left hand and ran a thumb over the wedding ring that her mother had once worn. The ring Josiah had produced when the preacher called for one. Right before the preacher declared them man and wife.

"You were staring at your ring as if it might poison you or some such. It's just a gold band, and a used one at that."

Maybe it wouldn't be so bad. Lots of women married men

they hardly knew. Look at all the women who had come out west as mail-order brides. It could be worse. She could have been forced to marry Jed. She suppressed the shudder that ran through her at that thought. Jed wouldn't have waited until they reached town to assert his husbandly rights. He probably would have taken her virginity as soon as they'd lost sight of the McLeod ranch, instead of taking her to a hotel for her wedding night.

Her wedding night. Where she'd have to do whatever her husband wanted. Accept whatever he was going to do with her without quarrel. She'd seen enough barn animals to know what to expect but the idea of Jackson mounting her, pushing his man parts inside her...she swallowed hard. She'd given her word she'd *honor and obey* him. Those words joined the *death do you part* phrase, creating a cacophony inside her head.

Jackson's fingers tightened around hers, and she realized his dark brows were drawn slightly together.

Her husband—how long before she got used to that phrase?—raised one dark eyebrow. "I asked if you were done eatin' and were ready to retire for the night."

Retire. To their room. *Their* room. Their bed.

"You don't need to be afraid of me, Miss Sarah. I ain't never forced myself on a woman."

He probably didn't have to force himself on any woman. She hadn't missed the second glances some of the women had spared him as he'd escorted her along the sidewalk when they'd first arrived. She couldn't put her finger on just what it was that made him so attractive. His nose had a bump in it as if it had been broken a couple times and not set right, his clothes were well worn, his boots scuffed. Perhaps it was his unassuming confidence that attracted her.

His lips pressed together, he pushed his chair back and

stood, holding out his hand to her. "The more you think about it, the worse it'll be in your head."

She placed her hand in his, wondering if he'd be repulsed by her calluses once she took her gloves off. The lady at the next table over with her fine linen dress with its lace bodice probably didn't have work-worn hands from shoveling out the barn, or hauling buckets of water not only for cooking and bathing but for the animals day in and day out. Neither did the other woman two tables over, the one with the blond ringlets and fancy bonnet with ostrich feathers who'd outright ogled Jackson when they were being shown to their table.

Jackson tucked her arm beneath his and leaned down to her, whispering, "You're prettier than either of them."

Reverend Glass would have chided her for sinning when a flush of both embarrassment and pride warmed her cheeks.

The walk up the stairs to their room went too fast. Too soon she was standing in front of the single big bed. He'd want her to undress and get into it. What if she didn't please him? She didn't know what a man expected when it came to satisfying them in the bedroom. *Oh Mama, why didn't you tell me what I needed to know about these things?*

Behind her, Jackson flipped shut the latch on the door, locking them in.

Was this how prisoners felt when they were locked in their cells for the first time? Her breath burning in her chest, Sarah wet her lips. What if he wanted her to do some of the things Jed had whispered? She tugged off her gloves and laid them beside her brush on the dressing table. Like her ring, they'd once been her mother's and bore the signs of age and use. Conscious of him watching her, she fiddled with the ribbons of her bonnet.

"You look scared to death. Do you really think I'll be that

mean to you?" Jackson took the bonnet from her and set it over her gloves.

"I'm f-fine." Her words might have held more weight if she hadn't stuttered.

"Nice try, but I ain't buying what you're tryin' to sell." He picked up her hands and chaffed them between his large palms. "Take a nice deep breath for me, will ya?"

Honor and *obey*. She sucked in a lungful and immediately regretted having that slice of peach pie for dessert. Her knees lost any sense of direction and wobbled beneath her, and the light from the kerosene lantern dimmed.

"Whoa. Stay with me, Sarah." He lifted her as if she weighed nothing and laid her on the bed. His face wavered at the edge of her vision, his eyes dark and concerned.

"Damned corsets. You can barely breathe, can you?" he growled.

"It's not the corset," she protested. "It wasn't done up that tight."

He glanced up at her, sat back on his heels, assessing her. What did he see? Fear? Did he realize it wasn't of him, but her fear of disappointing him, of not being enough. He shook his head. "Maybe not, but it's not helpin' is it?"

Without giving her a chance to argue, he bent his head and set to work on her stays like a man intent on solving a puzzle. Once he freed the last hook, she drew in a deep breath, one of the first she'd been able to take the entire day.

"Better?" The corset landed on top of her valise with a thud.

"Yes, thank you." But she grabbed the edges of her bodice together and wrapped her arms over her chest almost as tightly as the corset had squeezed her.

His lips pursed together into a hard line. "Whatever you're

thinking is going to happen is probably a hell— beggin' your pardon—a lot worse in your head than it will be in fact."

He was right. Something inside her quivered. Not in fear, but with an awareness she'd never known before. Her body softened, wanting to trust him, to rest against him and let him protect her. Her hands twitched, wanting to touch his shoulders, to play with the thin furring of hair on his chest and feel the strength of his muscles rippling in the dim light.

She took another deep breath. "All right. Let's get this over with." She stood up and grabbed the hem of her chemise.

"Now hang on a second." He captured her hands. It was the first time she'd seen him smile, she realized, and it changed his whole face. With that deep dimple in his left cheek, and the way his eyes sparkled, he looked like a little boy who planned to put a frog in her bed. "*Let's get this over with?* As much as a man likes to know a woman's willing, I'd rather not think of lying in our marital bed bein' a chore."

"I'm sorry." Maybe he wouldn't be able to consummate the marriage. Maybe he could only find satisfaction with a man in his bed. She dropped her eyes at the thought. No, from the bulge against his placket, he didn't need a man's touch to arouse him.

"Uh-uh, no apologies from you tonight. We'll take tonight right slow, all right?" He leaned back and tilted his head. "Sit down on that chair in front of the dressing table."

Bemused, she did as he bid. He stood behind her and removed the net covering her bun, then began plucking the pins holding her hair in its bun. "Let's start with this, shall we?" When she reached up to try to help him, he tapped her hands. "Nope, this pleasure's all mine. You just sit there."

He *hmm*'d as he removed more pins, freeing her hair from its rigid confines, letting it fall past her waist. "You've got beautiful hair. Why do you wear it all bound up so a man can't appreciate it?"

"Mr. McLeod insisted on it."

He met her gaze in the mirror. "Even when you were little?"

"Yes." Because when it was down, her Indian blood became even more obvious.

He made a disapproving noise in the back of his throat, then picked up the hairbrush she'd set out when they'd arrived.

She found herself relaxing with each stroke of the brush. She held her hand up, frowning at her mother's wedding ring now gracing her finger. "I wonder why he kept it all these years."

"Maybe because he still loved your ma." He continued brushing her hair in long smooth strokes. She'd never known a man to be so patient. "He stayed married to her, didn't he?"

"It's not like they had a choice. Any more than you today." She dropped her lids, eyeing him through her lashes. Would she find herself in the same type of loveless marriage?

"There's always a choice. Your father could have sent her to live somewhere else. Heck, with the land your pa owns, he could have built her a cabin at the far end of his land. Yet they stayed in the same house for another twenty some years, didn't they?"

But not the same room. In her whole life, she'd never seen her father touch her mother. Not until they had to move her from her bed to the table to be laid out.

"He let her stay because he needed a woman to do the household chores and help him raise Walt." He'd let her know often enough that was the only reason either of them had a roof over her head. "She didn't have anywhere else to go, so she didn't feel she had a choice either."

"Well, before you go doubting me, I had a choice. I could have saddled my horse and rode away. Not that I would have."

"Why not?"

"Because I gave my word." The brush paused midstroke. "I don't got much in this world, 'cept for my word. I break that, I ain't got nothing." He chuckled darkly. "Guess I shoulda mentioned that before we stood in front of the preacher."

He hunkered down in front of her, the brush loose in his hands. "I'm a ranch hand, Sarah. That's all I am. I don't own a house or any land. Now don't you worry," he rushed to assure her, "I got a little money saved up so you ain't gonna starve or be on the streets beggin' or nothin'. We're going to be stayin' at Nate's place at first, but I'm fixin' to find us a couple acres maybe, build us a house. It won't be a grand one. Probably won't be much more than a couple rooms at first, but we can always add on to it"—he stared at the brush, his cheeks tinged with color—"as we need."

If we have children, he was trying to say. "Oh."

While she loved the idea of cradling a babe in her arms, the thought of how that child would have to be conceived was both exciting, and frightening. Not to mention that any child of theirs would be subjected to the same painful taunts and scorn she'd endured all her life. Would they resent that she'd brought them into a world of rejection?

He swallowed and took a deep breath then placed her brush on the dresser. "Guess it's time for bed."

"Oh," she repeated, even quieter this time. The room suddenly shrank around her until all she could focus on was the bed. And Jackson.

He pulled her to her feet, then lifted her in his arms as if she weighed nothing. Before she could tense he was hushing her, crooning, "It's all right."

She found herself sitting on his lap on the bed, him cradling her once more, her crinoline billowing her skirt around them both.

"You know, it occurs to me you don't realize you might not be the only one nervous here."

Her laugh fractured in her throat. Him nervous? Who was he trying to fool? Except maybe she was the first woman he'd invited to his bed. What if he wanted Nate, not her? "So you have been with a woman before?"

He cupped his fingers beneath her chin, lifting it until she looked at him. "Yes, I've lain with women before. I just ain't never been with a vir—" His Adam's apple bobbed as he swallowed. Hmm, maybe he was nervous. "I ain't never been a woman's first before."

Reminded of her inexperience, Sarah dropped her eyes. What if he hurt her? Even unintentionally? What if she couldn't satisfy him? What if—

"Look at me, Sarah." His tone was gentle but compelling. "Have you been with a man before, sweetheart? Is that what you're worried about? That I'll realize I ain't your first?"

"I've never..." Her throat closed up, strangling her, so she could only shake her head.

His thumb stroked her wrist. For such a small gesture, she took heart that he could be gentle, soothing. Maybe it would be all right.

There was a long pause before Jackson sighed.

"Are you worried I'm gonna hurt you?"

"You're so big," she whispered. "Bigger than Jed."

His grip on her wrist tightened. "You want to explain to me how you know how *big* Jed is?"

"Because I've seen him." A shudder rippled up her spine as the memory of those incidents assailed her. "If he knew I was alone in the barn or in the house when he was visiting, he'd come in and...touch himself there."

"Did he ever touch you? Make you touch him?" Violence lurked just below the surface of the calm façade he maintained, betrayed by the knife-sharp question. And the rock-hard grasp on her arm.

"No!" She shook her head, her hair whipping from side to side with the ferocity of the motion. "But he'd tell me what he wanted to do to me. What he wanted me to do to him."

His grip on her wrist loosened. "Did you ever tell your pa —McLeod—about it?"

"I told my mother—she told Mr. McLeod. After that, he made sure I was never alone when Jed was around."

"At least he did somethin' right by you." His thumb started stroking again, the calluses strangely comforting. Beneath her, his thigh muscles relaxed, except for the hard lump at her hip.

She chanced a glance up at him and found him watching her, his lids hooded over dark eyes. If her heart had started to slow, it faltered and began its race once again. His hand released her wrist and cupped the back of her head, drawing her to him.

The first brush of his lips over hers had her tensing, but he didn't force himself upon her. His kiss was whisper-soft, a taste, a promise. She had the chance to draw in a single breath before he returned. This time he lingered, his lips firming against hers with an intensity that stole her breath.

"Kiss me, Sarah." His fingers stroked her hair, not pulling her closer, but not letting her retreat either. Still, he gave her the choice. "Trust me. Let me in."

She wasn't quite sure what *let me in* meant, but she leaned forward, resting a hand on his shoulder. After quickly wetting her lips, she leaned closer. She didn't immediately kiss him; instead, she hovered, enjoying his breath on her cheek, and the way his eyes closed, his lashes dark against his sun-ripened skin. The exotic pipe tobacco the man at the next table had been smoking still clung to his clothes, but beneath it, Jackson smelled of the soap he'd used when they'd cleaned up before dinner. And of something else, something warm and spicy.

With a groan, he closed the distance between them and caught her mouth. She gasped when his tongue swept across the seam of her lips. The moment her lips parted, his tongue darted inside, bringing with it a taste of the coffee he'd had. Is that what he'd meant by let him in?

He drew away, his breathing as heavy as hers.

"Let's get you out of the rest of this rig."

He made short work of the hooks and eyes her fingers had fumbled with when she'd dressed that morning. Her skirt pooled at her feet, joined shortly by the metal rings of her crinoline.

She would have been fine if he hadn't rested his hands on her hips and drawn her against him. The only thing separating her from the hard length resting against her belly was the thin cotton of her chemise and his trousers. No matter how hard she tried, she couldn't stop from stiffening in his arms.

"Don't you worry. We're gonna take this real slow tonight. " He made a soothing sound and returned to just kissing her. Even under such a simple attention, Sarah became aware of sensations rising in her body she'd never felt before. The way the chemise rasped against her nipples. The strange pulses heating her belly. Lower. Of how her body softened, how her breasts grew heavy, how each breath was hard to draw even without the corset confining her.

He stole another gasp from her when his hand cupped her breast, his thumb toying with the nipple the way she'd seen Nate playing with Jackson's the night before. The tips hardened into buds and he lowered his head over her breast. Never had she imagined the pleasure that poured through her when he captured the peak with his mouth. Heat from the tip through her belly and into the crevice between her thighs. Once again he made that soothing noise, the rumble from his chest accentuating the steady beat of his heart. Then he shifted so she lay on her back, staring up at him. Supporting himself on one elbow, he stared down at her, his eyes dark in the soft light, unfathomable. Callused fingers skimmed over her knee, up her thigh, then inward.

Her eyes opened wide, and she arched into the pillow with a gasp when his fingers slipped beneath the fabric and touched parts no man had ever dared touch.

"Sssh, stop thinkin' so hard and let yourself feel," he whispered.

Feel? How did she feel? Scandalous. Wanton.

Beautiful.

Beneath the cotton of her knickers, his fingers slipped between her folds and touched a spot that had her breath speeding up, catching in her chest in shallow pants. She had no idea what he was doing to her, but she craved...something. When she thought she'd find the answer to what she was seeking, he withdrew his hand. She almost cried out in disappointment.

He pressed a kiss to her forehead while his hands lifted her behind off the mattress and pulled her undergarments free. "Sit up, darlin'."

She moistened her lips again and took a deep breath before she sat up, the counterpane rough against her bare bottom. The nerves returned, the butterflies changed to frogs jumping in her stomach, or maybe they were rocks. Not breaking her gaze, he lifted the edges of her chemise and pulled it from her, leaving her completely naked and him completely clothed.

"So beautiful," he whispered, pressing her back against the pillows. He caught her hand and pressed a kiss to her palm, then placed it flat on her breast. "Have you ever touched yourself here, Sarah?"

Feeling the blood rush to her face, she nodded. "Sometimes."

"Show me what you like."

Until the night before, she'd only stroked them, but now she played with her nipples the way he had earlier. When his breathing hitched, she grew bolder and started rolling them between her thumb and forefinger. She gasped at the strength of the sensation, eliciting a chuckle from Jackson.

"Like that, do you?"

He shrugged out of his jacket and efficiently undid the buttons of his shirt. He slowed when he undid his trousers, almost as if he were shy. Or perhaps he was afraid he would shock her, frighten her by unveiling his arousal.

"It's all right," she whispered, the heat that had been fading from her cheeks flaring again. "I've already seen you, remember?"

He nodded, though his frown deepened.

Why did she have to remind him about that night in the barn? Of how his friend had touched him, aroused him.

Or perhaps he was remembering what she'd told him about Jed. She turned her head sideways and stared at the wall, all pleasure in what she'd experienced that night disappearing.

"I'm sorry. I didn't mean to remind you of Jed."

He sucked in a harsh breath. "That's not what I was thinking."

"Oh." So it *was* Nate he was remembering. Maybe if she

touched Jackson the way Nate had she could arouse him, make him forget the other man. Or maybe she'd never be good enough for him.

No. She had to try. Otherwise the marriage would fail, and they'd both be miserable.

The mattress dipped at her side and Jackson's hands touched her chin in an attempt to get her to face him again. "Look at me, Sarah."

She rolled her head back and discovered he was lying in the same position he had been before, up on one elbow, looking down on her. Except now he was naked, and his shaft was a hard heavy length jutting out from its nest of thick dark curls. The sight of it both excited her and scared her. She'd seen it engorged the night before, but now, so close, it seemed so much bigger. Would he expect her to do the things Jed had told her he'd do with it, put it places she was barely aware of? Would it hurt?

Jackson stroked her cheek, a gentle touch that relieved some of her fear. "I promise you, I'll not do anything you don't like. I give you my word of honor."

Though she'd known him for just over twenty-four hours, there was something in his voice that had her believing him. "Do you trust me?" She nodded.

His eyes crinkling, he kissed the tip of her nose. "Good girl." He picked up her hand, the one he'd originally placed on her breast, and moved it to the curls at the apex of her thighs. "Have you ever touched yourself here? When you were in bed maybe, all alone?"

"No." *Liar.* With a quiet sigh, she nodded. "Yes. Last night."

"After watching Nate and me?" He paused. "You weren't disgusted by us?"

"No." She swallowed hard. "I know I should have been, but..."

"But?"

"I imagined it was me lying there beside him. Me he was touching." Would that disgust him? "I overheard you talking about how Mr. Campbell had arranged for me to be his mistress, so I figured I'd be laying with him."

A strange look flickered across his face. Was he remembering Nate, wishing it were him in the bed instead of her? Or was he jealous that she'd pictured herself with Nate instead of himself?

"Nate had talked with McLeod about proposing to you himself, Sarah. You would have been his wife, not his mistress."

"Are you disappointed that you were forced to marry me instead?" Angry?

"No. I'll admit I was surprised to find myself in front of the preacher, but I am not disappointed. I hope you'll never find me wanting."

"I'm sure we'll muddle along just fine." Even she heard the doubt in her tone.

"Now best not to think about any of what happened last night and concentrate on what's happenin' here and now." He dipped his head to press a kiss into the spot where her neck joined her shoulder.

A shiver rippled down her body. Not that she was cold, but that spot sparked something in her, some need that had her hips lifting from the counterpane.

"Did you do what I was doing earlier? Like this?" His hand still covering hers, he slid her finger through her folds. They were wetter than they had been, and her fingers slipped through them easily.

"In a way. I touched myself...down there, but it didn't feel the same as what you did just now." *My body didn't burn the same way.*

He guided her fingers to places she'd not touched the night before, sliding them up and down, circling a spot that had her hips rotating against the pressure. A musky scent rose from the cream coating her fingertips. "Do you feel what's happening to your body, Sarah? Do you smell how aroused you are?"

"Yes." But she couldn't explain it. "It's like I need...something."

She cried out when he dipped his head and captured her breast with his mouth, his lips and tongue alternately sucking and soothing. Between the magic of whatever his fingers were doing and the exquisite sensations of him at her breast, her body floated, awash in sensations that frightened her, excited her. Confused her. She bucked beneath him when one of his fingers entered her, stroked a part that she didn't know existed, transported her to places she'd never been.

She lost track of time, letting herself drift as his fingers and mouth continued to pleasure her until part of her, deep inside, clenched and spasmed around his fingers, her breath leaving her lungs in a rush.

If he lived to be a hundred, Jackson thought he'd never see such a beautiful sight as Sarah lying beside him, her lips parted, glistening in the soft light. Her hair flowed over the pillow like a sheet of satin; a flush of arousal tinged her cheeks. Her breasts, with their tiny dark nipples, were perfect, just enough to fill his hand. Even though she'd already found her ease, her body rippled around his fingers, coaxing them deeper. Her warm cream coated his palm, her subtle womanly scent wafting up to entice him.

With a soft sound of contentment, her eyes opened and

focused on him. Her gaze skimmed over his chest stopping at his groin. "Is that what it'll be like?" Her

blush deepened. "When you're inside me?"

"If I'm doin' it right."

She took a shallow breath, her tongue darting out to moisten her lips, before she lifted her gaze to meet his. "May I touch you? Like you've touched me?"

He pulled his hand away from her and lay back on the pillows, allowing her unimpeded access to his body. "Touch me wherever you want. I'm all yours."

Her bottom lip caught between her teeth, she skimmed a finger across his shoulder. Her hand flattened as she traced down his breastbone, circling up to his nipples. She swallowed as she toyed with the tiny buds that puckered and hardened beneath her touch. To his surprise she dipped her head and caught one with her lips, nipping at it the same way he'd done to her earlier. Last night Nate had touched him with hard callused fingers, his grip sure, his body hard. Sarah's hands showed evidence of hard work as well, but the path they blazed as they trailed over his body left a different type of fire burning. Not better, not worse. Different. Equally hot and all-consuming.

That she touched him at all surprised the heck out of him, as had her admission she'd not been horrified by watching Nate touch him. Her curiosity about his body both intrigued him and aroused him in equal measure. Between the sensation of her teeth on his nipple and her hair draping over his chest, his dick hardened more than he'd dreamed possible. With a small turn of his head, he buried his nose in her hair. There was no fancy fragrance like the women he'd courted often bathed in, only the subtle perfume of the soap she'd used when she'd washed up mingling with her natural scent. He wouldn't have it any other way.

Her hand drifted over his belly, slowing when it reached the nest of hair at the base of his cock. He groaned when her fingers touched the sensitive shaft. It wasn't that he hadn't had a woman touch him there before, but there was something incredibly arousing about Sarah's innocent exploration.

He wrapped his hand about hers and closed her fingers around his shaft, showing her how to stroke him. She quickly learned what he liked, and soon his breath had turned to harsh pants.

His balls ached, but the last thing he wanted was to spend all over his own belly like a randy youth. But that meant being inside her. He'd heard tales of the pain a woman sometimes experienced her first time, and the last thing he wanted was to spook her by hurting her. She'd taken two of his fingers without pain. But there was also no denying his cock was thicker than his two fingers. Much thicker.

Beneath his hand, her thumb swirled over his sensitive head. Damn it, he couldn't wait any longer. He caught her hand by the wrist, stopping her. "Do you trust me, Sarah?" He couldn't help that his voice sounded more like a growl.

With no hesitation, she nodded.

He reached up and pulled her down to him, capturing her mouth in another kiss. As she relaxed her body over him, he shifted and rolled on top. Though she was tall for a woman, he was acutely aware of how small she was. Not fragile, just less wide of hips than most of the women he'd had, softer. Definitely more fragile than Nate.

Her arousal reached his nostrils, a spicy scent that promised to burst on his tongue in an explosion of flavors when he finally allowed himself that pleasure. Her dusky nipples thrust up at him, enticing him to suckle them.

He worked his way down her body, taking his time to make sure she'd be ready for him, exploring her soft belly, the curves of her hips, the bend of her knee. Despite her protests and the color flooding her face until it was as bright as a fresh-picked strawberry, he settled between the satin-soft skin of her thighs. He kept his eyes on hers as he ran his tongue through her folds, kissing and nibbling, discovering what made her breath hitch, what made her squirm, what made her groan. For a virgin, she was a surprise. She was sensuality wrapped in a beautiful package, promising pleasure for the rest of his life. Only once perspiration beaded her skin and she could no longer hold back the tiny whimpers did he act on his desires.

Holding his shaft in one hand, he positioned himself at her entrance. He'd done everything he could think of to ready her and uttered a silent prayer that he wouldn't hurt her. With a single flex of his hips, he pressed his shaft through the thin barrier at her entrance. He sucked in a breath when she winced and forced himself to stop his forward motion.

"Sarah? Are you all right?" Please God, don't ask him to stop, because she felt so fucking good around him, he didn't think he could pull out now.

In an infinite gesture of trust, Sarah wrapped her arms about him and pulled him deeper inside. Still he didn't move, letting her adjust to his girth. He nearly came undone when she started moving beneath him, a gentle undulation that caressed both his cock and his belly. He reached between them and stroked that spot he knew would give her pleasure.

He had to remind himself to go easy on her, remind himself that this was her first time and she'd be sore enough afterwards. But from the way she moved beneath him, the way her heels clamped onto his butt, holding him in place, he didn't seem to be hurting her.

Slow and easy, he glided back in until he was fully buried within her. He flexed his hips, alternating his strokes between shallow and deep. She gasped during one pass, her muscles tightening around his shaft. But was it from pleasure or pain? He glanced up and found her biting her lip.

"It's okay, darlin', you can make whatever noise you want. I need to know whether you like what I'm doin' or not."

"I like it," she choked out. "Do it again."

He flexed his hips, withdrawing from her. On the slow press in, her fingers dug into his forearms. Her soft gasp told him he'd found the sweet spot, especially when her movements became more frantic, her breathing ragged. Yup, she sure enough liked it right there. He filed away the knowledge for the future.

Soon he was thrusting, lost in the sheer pleasure of the way her sheath excited every inch of his cock. Any hesitation she'd shown at first disappeared, and she matched his passion stroke for stroke.

Between his rasping breath and her moans, and the way the headboard banged against the wall, anyone passing by in the corridor would have no doubt exactly what was going on in this room.

His hips ground against hers, and she stiffened beneath him. She was so close, but fear or embarrassment was stopping her from taking that leap. Her reached between them again and found her engorged bud, flicking it once, twice with his thumb.

With a long shuddering gasp, she climaxed, her body softening, heating around his cock in an embrace so tight he couldn't hold back. Need raced down his spine, bowing it as his balls drew up tight to his body. His seed jetted from him in long steady pulses, her sheath milking every last drop.

His lungs burning, he collapsed beside her. If he'd had any doubts that they'd suit when they were standing in front of the preacher this morning, she'd just removed one. When it came to the pleasures of the marriage bed, he had no doubt he'd done his duty.

Something inside him shattered when she rested her head on his shoulder and snuggled closer. Despite what she'd been through, what she still faced, she trusted him. A complete stranger.

She was a gift, one unexpected, unlooked for. One he would treasure forever.

CHAPTER 5

"It's been a pleasure to meet you, ma'am." The leader of the four Texas Rangers who had accompanied them touched the brim of his hat to Sarah before shifting in his saddle to face Nate. "You shouldn't have any problems from here, so if you don't mind, we'll leave you and head into town."

Nate shook the Ranger's outstretched hand. "Thanks, Carl. I appreciate you accompanying us all this way."

"My pleasure. My mama will be pleased to see me back around these parts. And she'll be right happy to hear there'll be a new member of the congregation to help her with the church socials." His gaze briefly slid to Sarah before returning to Nate. "As for that matter we discussed, we'll head back in the morning to check out your suspicions."

That her family had planned to steal back the horses, Sarah knew he was trying not to say. "Excuse me, but what will happen if you find proof that they have been rustling?"

"That'll be up to the circuit judge, ma'am."

If they made it to court. If anyone else discovered what they'd been doing, Walt and her stepfather might face a lynch mob. Sarah wasn't sure how she felt about the emotions tumbling inside her.

He touched his hat once more then held out a hand to Jackson. "Congratulations again, Kellar. You've got yourself a lovely bride. I expect there'll be a few ladies around town who will be disappointed you got yourself hitched."

After another glance in her direction, the four Rangers turned their horses and headed back to Barnett Springs.

"If anyone can get to the truth, it's Barnett and his friends, Miss Sarah," Nate said. "For all we know, your brother isn't guilty of anything more than shootin' the breeze." He clucked to his horse and urged it into a trot ahead of them.

Sarah clung to the reins until her knuckles whitened. No, they'd planned things too precisely for it to be idle chatter. That she may have just sentenced both McLeods to jail, or worse, sent a shiver running along her spine with spiked claws. If proof couldn't be found, would folks turn on her as an ungrateful hellion? After all, while Josiah had never had a kind word for her, he had fed her and clothed her while her mother was alive instead of casting her off, selling her to a whorehouse or leaving her on the steps of an orphanage the way others had muttered they'd have done.

"You did the right thing telling us about them." Jackson walked his horse until he was next to Bandit. "If that fella Jed had decided to meet us where you said, who knows what might have happened to you."

The gentle ferocity of Jackson's voice dispelled the coldness that had formed in her belly, replacing it with a warmth she'd grown to expect whenever he spoke to her. He wasn't angry at her but at her brother and father *for* her. The novelty of not being automatically blamed was almost overwhelming.

"What's so funny?" His scowl made him look even fiercer, yet she couldn't stop her smile from spreading.

"I'm not laughing at you." The words grateful, vindicated, comforted all floated to the surface when she searched for a way to describe why she was smiling, but she discarded each of them. None were exactly right. He waited, watching her with a hawklike gaze. When it became obvious he wouldn't be satisfied until she told him, she relented. "I cannot begin to tell you how happy it makes me feel that you believed me."

"Why wouldn't I? What reason would you have to lie?"

It was exactly the same argument she'd posed to her stepfather on numerous occasions she'd been blamed for something she hadn't done. Her smile faded. "I'm not used to being believed. Especially when it comes to something Walt's done."

The leather on his saddle creaked as he leaned across to stroke her cheek. "More proof McLeod is a fool."

He froze as if he'd just realized what he'd done, what he was doing. He pulled his hand back and set his horse in motion.

Sarah didn't bother to hide her smile this time—he wouldn't see it unless he glanced over his shoulder. This tall hard-looking man had a gentle side to him she'd not expected. Not only in their lovemaking in the hotel, but on the four days since. He'd constantly asked if she needed a rest when they'd been on the road for a while, especially that first day when he knew she'd been sore. He made sure she kept her water canteen filled and checked Bandit's hooves for stones at every stop.

Then there were the ways he found to touch her, the way his thumb would stroke her side that extra second longer than necessary when he helped her down off her horse at each rest stop. Or how he would place his hand at the small of her back when they'd walked along the sidewalk in Abilene, or to a bush when she'd needed privacy.

The nights when they'd had to make camp at the side of the road, he'd fussed over her comfort. Though he hadn't exerted his husbandly rights, the intimate touches continued beneath the cover of the blanket he pulled over them both. When they slept, she'd often awoken to find him curled around her, as though she were something precious to be protected.

They traveled another ten minutes before she broke the silence. "How much longer until we get to Nate's place?"

"We've been on his land pretty much since the Rangers left." They crested a hill. He pulled up his gelding, waiting until Bandit picked his way up the rocky path to his side. "You can see the roof of his house past those mesquites."

She stood in the stirrups to see through the opening between the trees. The house he pointed to had porches that ringed both levels, and gables decorated the eaves beneath the tiled roof. Whoever had built it had spent hours, and money, adding touches that spoke of love and pride. "It's bigger than ours—I mean the McLeods'."

"Sure enough is. Nate's parents built it, but he's made a few changes since he inherited it."

"It's much nicer than I expected. Bigger." What had she been expecting? They'd paid her father in cash, and the horses they rode were of good quality, as were their saddles.

She stared down at her worn and patched gloves. Jackson had bought her a new pair their first night in town, but she'd hated to get them dusty and worn before she'd even arrived at her new home. What would they think of her arriving in her homespun dress and repaired boots? Of her straight black hair that hung down her back in a single long braid, instead of being tucked into a more fashionable chignon?

Inside her gloves, her palms grew sweaty.

When she looked back at Jackson, his brows were drawn together. "I ain't gonna be able to afford to build a place as fine," he said. "You'll probably find yourself living in a log cabin with no new-fangled indoor plumbing or any of the amenities."

She was about to reply that she was used to outdoor plumbing and didn't need fine things when he glanced away, his lips thin lines from how hard he'd pressed them together. "I'm bettin' you're wishing McLeod made you marry Nate instead of me about now. I know I am."

If he'd slapped her in the face, it couldn't have hurt more. Annoyed that she'd misjudged him so badly, that she'd actually thought they might suit, Sarah set her heels to Bandit's flanks. Running away, not even sure where she was going, seemed more desirable than staying another place where she wasn't wanted. A moment later, horse hooves pounded on the track behind her, but she urged Bandit to lengthen his stride. She'd be damned if she'd give Jackson the pleasure of seeing the tears threatening to spill.

NATE JUMPED FROM THE SADDLE AND HANDED Annabelle's reins to one of the stable boys who'd come running at his approach. "Is your grandma around, Henry?"

"Yessir, she's in the kitchen." The boy's grin shone bright against his grime and sun-darkened skin. "She figured you and Mister Jackson would be back today, so she's been bakin' up a storm."

"She has, huh? She making biscuits?" His mouth watered at the thought.

Henry's head bobbed. "Yes, sir, and ribs too."

Grinning, Nate took the steps two at a time. His spurs jangled as he strode across the porch and stepped into the front hall. He inhaled a lungful of the heavenly scent filling the house. Nothing smelled as good as Miss Martha's cooking. His belly already growling its approval, he'd taken two steps when the kitchen door swung open.

"You stop right there and take your boots off, Nate Campbell." His housekeeper folded her arms and glared with that same look his mother had given him when he was six and he'd pried the chair rails off the walls—not only in his bedroom, but the entire upstairs hallway. "I just swept, and I'll not have you fillin' the house with your dust again."

"I'm going right back out in a minute." Nevertheless, he backtracked to the sisal rug outside the front door. "I thought you'd appreciate some warning that company's coming."

"Oh, lordy, boy, who have you brought home this time? It better not be Miss Eliza after the way she treated you last Christmas."

He winced at the memory of Eliza's reaction when he hadn't given her an engagement ring as she—and her mother— had expected. "No, not Eliza. Jackson's got himself hitched while we were away, so I've invited him and his...wife"—would that word ever not stick in his throat?—"to stay."

"Hitched. Jackson?" Martha stilled, her eyes searching his expression which he struggled to keep bland. "He didn't get roped in by one of those painted ladies over in Austin, did he? Or some wilting flower from back east?"

"No, ma'am, neither of those. It's a long story and they'll

be along shortly, but I think you'll like Miss Sarah." To back up his words, hoof beats pounded in the distance, coming closer.

To Nate's relief, the impending arrival of company distracted Martha's examination of him. She whipped off her apron as she disappeared into the kitchen.

Moments later she returned, one hand smoothing her skirts, the other fiddling with the crocheted net holding her hair in place. "Am I presentable?"

"Of course." He held open the screen door, and they both waited on the porch as Sarah raced toward the house, Jackson's gelding hot on Bandit's heels.

When she saw Sarah galloping down the lane on Bandit, Martha cuffed the back of Nate's head, knocking his hat to the ground. "You made her ride on horseback all the way? You couldn't have at least hired a coach or taken the train?"

"It's her own horse she's riding." Nate stooped to pick up his hat and banged it against his thigh, knocking off the dust. "Plus, Jackson had to help with the other horses. Besides, she said she'd rather ride horseback than be cooped up in a coach."

Martha harrumphed in displeasure. "Of course, she'd say that, bless her heart. A new bride worth her salt wouldn't want to be a burden on her husband, would she? Shall I put her in the bedroom where Jackson keeps his things?"

Not *Jackson's bedroom*. That they hadn't managed to fool her as to where Jackson slept should not have been a surprise. Nate whispered a prayer of thanks that Martha hadn't publicly decried their behavior. "I think that would be best."

Nate jumped from the porch as Sarah pulled Bandit up in front of them. He caught Bandit's bridle and held the stallion as Sarah swung from the saddle. "Welcome to the Circle Star, Miss Sarah."

"Thank you kindly, Mr. Campbell." Sarah dropped into a

polite curtsey. When she rose, she placed her gloved hand in his in a move that made Nate's breath catch.

If only McLeod had listened to his argument, then Sarah would be walking up the steps as his wife, calling him Nate. Following him to his bedroom— their bed. Instead he'd have to keep his distance from her while pretending he wasn't aroused by her grace.

"Your home is lovely." She swallowed several times. "Thank you for letting us stay here until we find a place of our own."

Upon closer inspection, Nate realized her eyes were red. She'd been crying. Shit. Had she just realized she'd probably never see her old home again? Jackson's glower was black as thunder—his eyes narrowed to slits, and his eyebrows drawn so there wasn't but a sliver of skin between them.

Damn it, Nate cursed to himself. He'd left them alone for fifteen minutes, twenty tops, and they'd managed to have a spat?

Damning McLeod once more for turning him down, he tucked her hand beneath his elbow and walked her to where his housekeeper waited. "Mrs. Martha Simons, I'd like you to meet Jackson's bride, Sarah." He helped her up on the porch. "Miss Martha here drops by from time to time to keep me in line. If Jackson's lucky, maybe you'll be able to convince her to divulge the recipe to the sauce she uses on her ribs."

Martha must have caught the tension between the newlyweds as well, because a furrow appeared in her forehead and her tone was cool when she nodded to Sarah. "Welcome to the Circle Star, Miss Sarah. Why don't you come inside while the men take care of the horses?"

Nate stayed where he was, waiting until Sarah followed Martha into the house before he rounded on Jackson. "She was fine when I left you two alone. What did you do to upset her?"

Jackson swung out of the saddle. He tossed Thunder's reins to Henry's brother Clint, growling instructions to walk him a few minutes more. He waited until the boy was out of earshot before he spoke again. "She's got her drawers in a twist because I told her I wouldn't be able to afford to build a place like this."

"Nah, I can't see Miss Sarah being all uppity and expecting fine things." Not like that money-grasping harridan Eliza had turned out to be. "You must have said something else."

Jackson stared at the front door. "Damn it, Nate, all I said was that I wouldn't be able to afford a place as fine as this, and that she probably regretted being married to me instead of you. Next thing I knew she was riding off hell bent for leather like I was the devil on her heels."

There had to be another explanation. "Maybe she's afraid she'll never see her family again." Though given their behaviour he doubted that was true.

"I told her right off I'd let her go back to visit if she wanted. She didn't seem anxious to take me up on my offer. You saw the way they treated her. I don't know what bee got in her bonnet, but then I never did understand women." He took off his hat and thwacked it against his thigh. "Have Martha make sure she gets settled. I'm going to go help Clint with Thunder."

Left alone on the porch, Nate stared at Jackson's back as he retreated to the barn. "You damned fool."

Sarah followed Martha, barely hearing the woman as she pointed out various rooms and features of Nate's house. The heels of her boots clicked across the spotless loblolly pine floors. She'd offered to take them off but Nate's—housekeeper? Distant aunt? Family friend?—had waved her off and immediately started her tour.

Miss Martha finally wound down. "You must be plum tuckered out, and here I am going on to beat the band." She opened the solid plank door. "This is the guest room. I imagine you and Jackson'll do fine here."

The guest room proved to be a room bigger than her mother's bedroom. A massive rope bed took up most of the space. A set of green gingham tiebacks held open the matching drapes, letting the afternoon sun light the room. As she examined the room she realized it gave her no sense of who Jackson was. There were no pictures on the wall, no beloved knickknacks he'd treasured since childhood or mementos of family. There wasn't even a brush or a shaving set on the wash stand. Despite the lack of adornments, it was the type of room she could imagine waking up in each morning. But given Jackson thought her a burden, would it turn into a haven or a hell?

"I doubt Mr. Nate'll mind if you want to fix it up to your own tastes. This place needs a woman's touch." Martha frowned. "I didn't see a trunk or anything on any of the horses the boys brought back. Are your things being brought in by buckboard or somethin'?"

How did she explain that everything she owned had been packed in Bandit's saddlebags without appearing a pauper?

Martha must have guessed the reason behind her embarrassment, maybe from the heat creeping up Sarah's neck, because she patted her hand. "Ah, don't you worry about a thing, honey. Jackson will see that you have everything you need." She pulled her hand away and fiddled with the net holding her hair in place. "So how'd you two end up married?

He didn't say a thing about it before they left." Martha's face didn't lose its smile, but Sarah heard the circumspection in her tone.

Before she could stop herself, the tale started tumbling out, though she carefully kept to herself Jackson and Nate's relationship. She ended with, "He didn't want to marry me, but now he's stuck with me because Josiah refused to believe Jackson hadn't touched me."

"Funny, here I've been thinking about how you might be regrettin' being stuck with *me*."

Sarah whipped around to find Jackson standing in the doorway, her saddlebags in his hand. "I didn't hear you come in."

His mouth twitched up at one side and he gestured with his free hand to his sock feet. "Miss Martha always insists we take our boots off at the front door. Says she has enough dust blowin' through this place without us trompin' in more." He glanced down at her boots. "Guess she likes you more than us."

He hung his hat on a hook by the dresser before handing the saddlebags to Martha. "Those are Sarah's clothes. I suspect they're gonna need an ironing before she can put them on."

Martha huffed. "They'll need a good airing too, if they've been stuffed in here for the whole time. I'll take her into town next day or so for fabric so we can make her some more clothes too."

"These are fine. And I can hang up my cl—," Sarah started to say, only to be cut off by Jackson.

"You'll be busy with me." He cupped Martha's elbow and led her to the bedroom door. "If you'll excuse us, Miss Martha, I think I'd like to clean up a bit myself. And I need to talk with my wife for a moment about a matter between us."

"Of course." Martha patted his arm with an ease that Sarah envied.

Jackson had shrugged his suspenders off his shoulders and let them drop to his side, when a young boy no more than ten peeked his head in the door. "Gramma said to bring you some fresh water, Mr. Jackson."

"Here now, you should knock before walkin' into a room. You've been raised better than that." Despite his gruff tone, Jackson took the filled pitcher from the youngster's hands and ruffled his hair. "You go out and help your brother cool off the horses. Make sure he don't give them too much grain."

"You can count on me. Those mares are right fine lookin' fillies." The boy's face lit up, and he raced down the hall, calling instructions to his brother.

Once the door closed behind her, Jackson undid the buttons of his shirt. He tugged it over his head and let it flutter to the bed, leaving him in his undershirt. A moment later, it joined his shirt on the comforter.

Sarah found the play of muscles over his shoulders and back fascinating. She'd seen men out in the fields working on the fences and such, but they'd always pulled on their shirts before they'd come up to the house. Being so close to a man without his shirt on— to Jackson specifically—did strange things to her insides, as her body remembered all those wild and wanton things he'd done when he'd shown her what it meant to be a wife, a lover. Until she remembered that he didn't want to be married to her.

Jackson poured some water into the washbowl. After dampening the wash cloth, he scrubbed it over his face and neck so hard she was surprised he hadn't removed the top layer of skin. When he finally spoke, his voice was gruff. "Why do you think I regret being married to you?"

"Because you said you wished I'd married Nate, not you. I thought if we gave ourselves some time we might suit, but you're not even giving me a chance, are you?"

His jaw dropped for a moment before he turned back to the ewer. With a soft curse, he tossed the washcloth in the bowl. "I meant you would have been *better off* with Nate instead of me. Not that I regret marryin' you."

Before she could move, he'd crossed the floor and cupped his hand beneath her jaw. His touch was gentle, as if she were a bird or a delicate object he might break. "I would have liked to have done the deciding and askin' myself instead of bein' forced by McLeod to take marriage vows, I can't deny it. But I'll do my best to do right by you, you hear? I may not be able to build you as big a house or furnish it with things as fine as this one, but I'll never regret that you're my wife. "

"Then stop apologizing for what you can't give me." She leaned her cheek into his palm. "In case you hadn't noticed, I didn't have much at Mr. McLeod's home, either."

"You always call him Mr. McLeod. In all these years, he never let you call him Pa or Pop or some such?"

She shook her head. "I'm the living reminder that his wife cuckolded him. Would you accept another man's child as your own?"

"I'd like to think I'd man up to my responsibilities. It ain't the child's fault who her parents are. Or aren't." His hand left her jaw to play with a tendril of hair that had fallen in her wild ride. "What about your mama? She must have loved you."

"She said she did. When no one was around, she used to call me her special gift."

Maybe he heard the sorrow in her voice, because he frowned and asked, "And when others were around?" Sarah dropped her gaze. "Then she'd say I was God's way of punishing her for her sins."

Jackson cursed under his breath. "Given the way McLeod treated you, she was probably saying it to keep him happy. Miss Martha does that to keep her husband happy when he's ornery."

Ornery. That described Mr. McLeod to a T. And Jackson was right, her mother loved her—when they were out of Josiah's sight.

Would she find herself resorting to such measures now she was married too?

His brows drew even closer together. "I don't want you doin' that to me, you hear? Next time you have a problem with somethin' I do, or somethin' I say, you come out and tell me. I ain't McLeod or Miss Martha's Abner so you don't have to worry about me hittin' you or nothing. I promise."

"I won't have to see Mr. McLeod again. Will I?" He shook his head, his expression softer somehow.

"Not unless you want to."

"I don't."

"Then that's settled. You're mine. All mine." He bent his head and brushed his lips over hers. Her eyes fluttered closed as the heat in her belly spread upward. And lower. Surely he could hear her heart thumping against her ribs or knew how her blood raced so close to the surface.

With deft fingers, he unbuttoned her bodice and spread the fabric wide. She sucked in a breath when he unhooked her corset and pulled it from her.

"I thought I told you not to wear one of those while we were riding."

"I didn't know who I'd be meeting when we arrived. I wanted to make a good impression."

"Aw, darlin', any person who judges you by what undergarments you wear ain't worth worryin' about."

When his hand cupped her breast, she leaned into him with a soft sigh. He deepened the kiss, parting her lips with his tongue. It had been strange the first time he'd done it, but she'd found she enjoyed it. Especially when he kissed her like that at the same time he played with her breast.

She leaned full against him by the time he broke off the kiss.

"I'm thinking maybe you need proof that I don't mind being married to you."

She already had the proof, if the erection pressing into her belly was an indicator.

He undid her riding skirt with a murmured, "You wear too many clothes." Her chemise was quickly drawn over her head, her knickers pushed over her hips leaving her naked, vulnerable. His gaze raked her from the top of her head to her stockinged feet. "I've been thinking about doing this all day."

He had?

With that, he dipped his head again. Instead of kissing her mouth, this time he laid a series of soft kisses down her neck until she was trembling. When he captured one nipple with his mouth, she had to hang on to his shoulders with both hands.

Her whole body seemed connected somehow. Her mouth, her neck, her breasts, and parts of her body she'd barely been aware of before. Secret parts. The first night they'd been together he'd called it her pussy—maybe because he liked stroking it, she wasn't sure. All she did know was that when he touched her like this, her pussy and other parts of her body, deep inside, ached in a way she'd never experienced before.

He pressed her onto the feather mattress and parted her legs, exposing her private parts to him, but she'd learned that very first time not to try to cover it from him. "You have such a pretty pussy. It's all swollen and glistening, waiting for me to taste it like a fresh picked plum."

Her cheeks must have been the same color as a plum the first time he'd put his mouth down there. Even now, knowing what he would do, she felt the blush creeping over her chest, up her neck and flooding her face.

He undid his belt, then unbuttoned his trousers and let them drop; his belt buckle hit the floor with a clank. His erection was stiff against his underclothes, a hard ridge that still startled her. He wasted no time in stepping out of his drawers before kneeling on the bed between her outspread knees.

His fingers feathered light trails up the inside of her thighs. "Have you been thinking about this, Sarah? About us bein' in a real bed tonight? About me doin' this to you?"

Aware that her breathing was shallow, shaky, she nodded. Was it scandalous for a woman to admit? Would he think her her mother's daughter for such thoughts?

"Good. I'm glad." His hands found her lower lips and parted them. It felt so strange, so wonderful.

He should let her get dressed. Take her out to the kitchen and feed her. From the smells wafting down the hall and the sounds of cutlery clanking, Martha was setting the table, which meant the meal would soon follow. But now he knew what had set Sarah off, he needed this. To remind her that despite what she'd thought he said, he desired her as a woman, that he didn't feel saddled to her. To ease that part of him that demanded he claim her as his own.

Her skin was so soft beneath his fingers, though her thighs were muscular. No doubt from the riding she'd done. It had damned near scared him to death when she'd insisted on riding that high-spirited stallion Bandit. But she'd proven to be an excellent horsewoman, never letting the horse forget who was in charge.

He dragged his thumb between her glistening folds again. Her body rippled and tightened with each stroke. Her eyelids fluttered closed as she gave in to his attentions. She was so responsive to even the gentlest touch. What more could a man ask from his wife?

Wife. He still wasn't used to the concept, but damned if he wasn't going to enjoy its benefits.

He lowered his mouth to her juncture and allowed himself a taste of her. Moisture coated his tongue as he lapped at her folds. Now he'd had a taste of her spicy musk, he'd never get it out of his head. And from the way she was moving her hips, pressing her sweet pussy into his face, she was enjoying herself as well.

Alternating between lapping and nipping at that tight little bud hidden in her folds, Jackson paid close attention to her moans. His chin was coated in her juices when he slid his first finger into her. She groaned as her muscles clamped around him, drawing him deeper.

"Jackson, please." Her voice was low and husky, her plea unmistakable as her hands clenched his hair as though she thought she might float away if she didn't hold tight.

"I gotcha."

A second finger joined the first, pumping slowly against her sensitive front wall. He continued the movement with his fingers, concentrating on driving her wild with his tongue, teasing that sensitive nerve bundle until her body stiffened. She didn't scream her release like some of the women he'd bedded, but the sounds she was making could probably be heard clear down to the kitchen.

They were definitely being felt clear down to his balls. As

soon as her legs relaxed, he withdrew his hand. He positioned the head of his cock and slid into her warm, still-pulsing pussy.

His breath caught in his throat when her muscles clamped around his shaft, holding him in. Holy hell in a bucket, that first wave hadn't been her climax. That had just been the lead-up.

His world reduced to the bed, to Sarah's face scrunched up and eyes closed as she rode out her orgasm. Sweet mercy, he couldn't stop himself from rearing up and thrusting deeper, withdrawing and plunging deep again. Her legs wrapped tight around his hips, her arms straining to drag him down to her.

Their lips fused together, her hands streaking over him, touching, exploring until he was mindless. He'd never known such a craving. Both his and hers. He drove her, ruthless in his quest to watch her—feel her—orgasm again. When she bucked beneath him, demanding more, urging him to be rougher, harder, he growled and complied.

No wilting miss, not his Sarah. She was his match. Strong. Vital. Challenging. She gave as good as she got, her fingers digging into his ass cheeks. The bite of pain from her fingernails threatened to send him over the edge, but he was damned if he'd come without her.

He moved from her neck where he'd buried his face to her breast and captured one of those dark plump buds with his teeth, nipping just enough that it might sting for a bit. He flattened his tongue and soothed the sting, then repeated the process all over again until her body stiffened beneath his. One thrust, another and she shattered, taking him with her.

CHAPTER 6

Horses and carriages filled the town square that had been almost empty when Sarah had ridden through it the week before. Farmers stood in groups, no doubt talking about last year's crops or perhaps speculating about the upcoming season. A dozen stalls had been set up in the center by a few hopeful peddlers braving a brisk wind, winter's final gasp.

Once Nate stopped the carriage, he jumped down and tied off Bandit. Sarah clambered from the carriage and stood beside him. He tucked her hand in the crook of his arm.

"It was really nice of you to bring me into town today."

"I had to come in anyway." He gestured with his chin along the raised boardwalk. "The dress shop is half a block down."

"I can buy fabric and make my own dresses," she protested. "They'd be cheaper and more practical."

His lips flattened. "I'm paying so don't go for the cheapest fabrics. Get yourself more than one dress too. Practical is fine, but get yourself something pretty too."

"But—" Wouldn't it look strange to everyone else to have a man who wasn't her husband paying for her clothes? Might they think she was a kept woman, cheating on her husband before the marriage had even begun?

"Let me do this for you, Sarah. Think of it as a welcome to Barnett Springs, or maybe a wedding present for you."

He was so naturally good-natured she had to smile. "Thank you. But maybe you could mention that to the seamstress so tongues don't wag?"

"Tongues will wag no matter what, Sarah. Don't let what other people think sway your choices."

"Besides, both Miss Martha and Jackson made me promise to make sure you buy some new gowns. And they're powerful hard people to ignore when they get an idea in their heads."

Jackson. Would she ever get to a point where she didn't feel like the third person in the relationship? "You'd do anything for him, wouldn't you?"

Nate stopped walking and turned to face her. "Of course—he's my best friend. But I would have offered to bring you along anyway."

He would have brought in a stranger if he'd been asked, she realized. She'd hit him and kneed him. And then taken his best friend—his lover—from him. "When I came into the barn that night I had no idea I'd end up coming between you. I've not had a chance to apologize to you for that."

He glanced away, his expression shuttered. "It was probably for the best. He's the only man who I've ever felt *that way* about, and I was starting to take chances around him that I shouldn't have. I don't blame you, if that's what you're worried about."

He met her gaze once more. How many men would have been so honest with her about himself?

"But make no mistake, Sarah," he continued, "I would have been proud to have stood beside the preacher with you if

McLeod had let me. I would have tried to be a good husband to you."

His sincerity warmed her heart. She thanked whatever had led them to the McLeod ranch that day. If they hadn't, she'd never believed men such as them existed.

As they started walking toward the dressmakers, Sarah wondered what it would be like to have married Nate instead of Jackson. He was good natured and would have treated her kindly, she was certain. He was definitely handsome though in a different sort of way than Jackson, whose rugged looks created a charm of their own.

Nate had dressed for town, abandoning his farm clothes. His fashionable wool great coat must have set him back quite a few dollars, as had his tooled leather boots. But he wore them so casually she hadn't felt like a drab little mouse, until a woman wearing a moss-green silk gown beneath a matching velvet cloak stopped in front of them.

"Good mornin', Mr. Campbell." She twirled a lacy parasol that matched the ivory bows on both her cloak and her bonnet. This was the type of woman Nate deserved to walk down the street with.

"Afternoon', Miss Eliza." Nate tipped his hat at the woman. Sarah wondered that he didn't smile back at the woman, and at the way his arm tensed beneath her fingers. "Miss Eliza Owens, may I introduce you to Mrs. Sarah Kellar, Jackson's wife, and a good friend of mine."

"Jackson's *wife?*" The woman's gaze was sharp, matching her tone. "At least he's given up chasing after us God-fearing white women and sticking to his own kind."

"Shrew," Nate muttered just loud enough for Sarah to hear.

Heartened by Nate's comment, Sarah stiffened her spine

and met the woman's cool gaze. She'd be darned if she'd say it was a pleasure to meet this harridan.

"If you'll excuse us, Miss Eliza." Nate covered Sarah's hand with his and led her away, leaving the woman staring after them. "Sorry about her, Miss Sarah. Most folk in Barnett Springs aren't so narrow-minded."

"I'm used to it, don't worry about me." His annoyance on her behalf made it easier to slough off.

"Let's get you out of this wind. That coat's not fit for this weather." Nate sheltered her with his body and led her to a store proclaiming the latest in ladies' fashion. "Miss Martha said you needed new gowns, and she's right. So we're not leaving here until you buy at least three."

He signaled to a clerk, who hurried to their side. Sarah gaped when he gave the clerk instructions to bring out a variety of her best fabrics and patterns for them to examine.

Horrified at the amount of money the fabrics would cost Jackson, Sarah turned to the woman now in the process of measuring her. "Just show me some plain fabrics. Some cottons and wools."

With a sideways glance at Nate, who nodded, the clerk pulled out bolts of fabric that Sarah deemed much more affordable. Once she'd made her choice, Nate led her to the mercantile. While he placed an order for some new pump he claimed could be installed in the house, she fingered a pair of soft kid gloves decorated with a finely embroidered spray of violets. The pair she wore, though repaired in multiple places, were serviceable enough for a while longer, she decided, trying to ignore the stab of regret when she put them down. She wandered to a display of women's hats, where she fell in love with a totally impractical velvet bonnet adorned with ruched silk ribbons and a jaunty ostrich feather.

"You should buy it," Nate encouraged, startling her from her dreams.

She shook her head. "It's too expensive. The one I have may be plain, but it's warm."

He huffed in exasperation. "Jackson'll be upset to find you've not bought anything but cheap cottons and rough wools. He can afford it, you know. That's why he wanted you to come with me into town."

"I don't need fancy things, Nate. What I've ordered shall do me just fine."

"Then at least let me buy you that pair of gloves you were admiring."

He'd been watching her try them on? She glanced back at the gloves, sorely tempted, but shook her head. "I don't need anything more. But I thank you for your offer. It was very kind."

"You are one of the stubbornest women I've ever met." He checked his pocket watch and stared at the sky. "It's going to rain. Maybe even snow. We'll have to come back to the market next month."

Once again he tucked her hand in the crook of his arm and led her back to the square. As they approached the carriage, they had to step around three men admiring Bandit.

"That sure is a mighty fine lookin' stallion you've got there, Campbell. How much would you charge for him to cover my Ladybird?" A heavy-set man with a greying handlebar moustache stroked Bandit's neck, his eyes bright in appreciation.

"Well, now, it's not me you should be talking to, Colonel. Bandit is Miss Sarah's horse."

Sarah jerked in astonishment. "But you—"

"Tell you what, Colonel, why don't you come out to the

Circle Star tomorrow morning, and she and her husband can discuss stud fees with you then?" Grinning at Sarah, who raised an eyebrow at him, Nate touched the brim of his hat and handed her into the carriage.

Once they were trotting down the road, Sarah tugged at Nate's arm. "Why did you say Bandit's mine? You bought him from Mr. McLeod. I know what you paid for him. He's yours."

"No, he's yours. Always has been."

"You can't just give away something that valuable. And not to me, another man's wife. What would people think?"

"Aw, hang what others think. I can give you anything I want." He held up a hand when she started to object. "You've been nothing but gracious to me and Jackson, especially considering what you saw that night."

"So this is about my silence?"

"No!" He gentled his voice. "This is about you being my best friend's wife. Think of it as a wedding present, if it makes you feel better. Take his stud fees and put them towards whatever you want. That hat you liked, maybe."

A wedding present.Weren't the gowns the seamstress was making his wedding present? There had to be some catch. "What do you get out of it?"

"I get the pleasure of seeing a good woman smile."

Her eyes searched his, deep unfathomable pools that held no judgment, and no expectation of something in return. She leaned closer and pressed a kiss to his cheek. "Then both Jackson and I thank you for your wedding presents. You're a good man, Nathaniel Campbell."

A good man? A *good* man, Nate told himself, wouldn't be jealous of his best friend. A good man wouldn't be picturing turning his head and capturing his best friend's wife's mouth and kissing her senseless.

The sun hung low on the horizon by the time they returned to the Circle Star ranch. Jackson waited for them on the front porch. He strode down to meet them, lifting Sarah from the carriage.

Jackson hefted the bundle from the dress shop and tucked it under his arm while escorting Sarah into the house. Nate kept his lids lowered in an attempt to hide how he watched the gentle swing of Sarah's skirts. It wouldn't do to be caught ogling another man's wife.

He hadn't lied when he said he would have been proud to take his vows as her husband. Though it left him disturbed that he still fantasized about being in bed with Jackson, Sarah had been appearing in those fantasies lately.

While the couple disappeared upstairs, Nate headed for the kitchen. He paused at the tiny bouquet of flowers in a cup by Sarah's chair. Neither of them had missed the tears sparkling in Sarah's eyes when Jackson had picked a flower the first day they were on the road and handed it to her. Though she'd not said anything, they'd both figured no one had ever given her flowers before. Each day since, Jackson had made it a habit of bringing her a flower home, sometimes delaying their return from the fields to find one.

Maybe that's why he'd purchased the gloves she'd tried on, and that silly hat with its feather bobbing high in the air. And a heavier cloak—not a fancy one like Eliza had worn, but a serviceable one he knew would keep the wind and the rain away from Sarah. All right, and maybe he'd gone overboard by ordering three dresses special-made, but the fabrics she'd purchased were too plain, too dreary She needed pretty things. She deserved pretty things.

His stomach grumbling, he'd set the table and was about to call them for dinner by the time Sarah and Jackson joined him.

Sarah stopped in the middle of the room, her mouth dropping briefly as she stared at the table. "Was Martha here earlier?"

"Nope." Nate felt his color rise in his cheeks as he held her seat for her. What did she think he was? Helpless? "You think I ain't capable of settin' a table or makin' dinner?"

"No, of course not."

He remembered that none of the McLeod men had lifted a fat finger to serve themselves when they'd stayed over, instead insisting Sarah serve them like she was a goddamned servant. It rankled that she might lump him in the same category as those louts.

"A couple of Rangers stopped in earlier." Jackson straddled his chair beside Sarah and stabbed his fork into the cold slab of Sunday's roast beef Nate had placed in front of him. "Said they've heard back from Barnett and his boys. Looks like there have been other reports of other farmers who made a deal with McLeod, only to have their cattle or horses stolen from them afterward."

Nate grabbed the coffee jug and poured himself a mug. After a moment's thought he filled mugs for Jackson and Sarah as well and set them in front of them before taking his seat at the table. "Why hadn't the local sheriff cottoned onto their game before?"

"Looks like they targeted non-locals and attacked their targets on county boundaries. No one had put it together before. They went to the ranch to question McLeod but he weren't nowhere to be found."

He'd grown to enjoy dinner time, using the opportunity to surreptitiously observe both Jackson and Sarah.

When they finished the meal, Jackson stood, his chair scraping across the wood floor. He glanced at Sarah then held Nate's gaze. "Sarah? Why don't you go sit by the fire? We've got this."

She glanced up, clearly startled. "But—"

"Nope, no arguments. You've made dinner and cleaned up after us all week. We've got this one." So Jackson had caught his message.

Nate stood and grabbed his plate and started piling the others onto it. "That's right, Sarah. We're not totally incompetent in the kitchen. We managed to feed ourselves and clean up before you married this fella. Won't do to dote on us too much, it'll make us lazy."

Her lips twisted up in a smile that told him she knew exactly what they were doing. "Thank you. I was fixin' to do some knitting anyway. Now I'll be able to grab the light while it's still good."

Before she'd come to live with them, he and Jackson would sit by the fire, Jackson repairing some bridle or other. Or he'd bring in the books and sit at the table, the way they were now. The only change was the click of Sarah's needles, and the sheer contentment Nate found in their company.

Too soon, Sarah put her knitting in her lap and yawned. Nate squelched his regret when Jackson stood up and the couple wandered upstairs, their arms linked. A few minutes later, he closed his eyes when Sarah's laughter floated down the stairs. He buried his head in his arms at the rhythmic squeaking of the bedframe. It wasn't right that he begrudge his friend the pleasures of the marital bed.

If he could only figure out if he was jealous of Jackson. Or of Sarah.

Nate stared at the water rippling in the ewer on the nightstand. There was no mistaking what was going on in the spare bedroom. Not from the way the bedframe hit the wall or the moans—both Jackson's and Sarah's.

Wasn't it enough he'd gone to sleep last night listening to the two of them knocking boots? He shouldn't have to wake up to the same sounds this morning.

He shut his eyes, but by shutting out the room, his imagination supplied an image of Jackson—coated in a sheen of sweat, the muscles of his thighs and ass flexing and rippling with strength. Damn, it had been over a month since he'd had Jackson's hard body covering him, his even harder cock trapped between their bellies.

On the other side of the wall, Jackson said something, his tone dark and commanding. Though distance and lumber prevented him from hearing the actual words, the timbre of Jackson's voice made Nate groan. He stumbled to the bed, taking the time to undo the belt he'd just buckled, and dropped his trousers before he fell onto the feather mattress. His hand closed around his already primed cock, his mind confused over who he pictured doing this for him. A month ago, it would have been Jackson's hand. Now it was Sarah's hand he envisioned clasping him. Nate ran his thumb over the swollen head and tried not to picture the couple on their bed. Which meant that was all he could see.

Pretty Sarah and her long black hair that Jackson had helped her brush out every night they'd been on the trail. Hair that Nate imagined cascading over his arms, his chest as she rode him with the ease she rode Bandit. Did they follow the same ritual in the privacy of their bedroom? Was it a form of foreplay for Jackson when he was with a woman?

Was she riding Jackson? Or was Jackson on top? Was he looking into those beautiful dark eyes that missed nothing? Or was she face down, her ass in the air while Jackson mounted her like a stallion?

Nate matched his strokes to the rhythm of the thumps on the wall, paying extra attention to the swollen, sensitive head when Sarah's moans got louder. His hips pushed his shaft into his palm at another of Jackson's murmured instructions. What would it be like to be in Sarah's pussy while Jackson's cock filled his ass?

Damn it, what type of man fantasized about fornicating with them both at the same time? Yet once the images started flowing, he couldn't stop. Sarah on her knees in front of him, his cock in her mouth, Jackson's hard body behind him, his cock rigid in his ass. Or him on his knees, his mouth on Sarah's pussy—she'd taste like heaven, he was certain—with Jackson pounding into him from behind. Him on his knees, his mouth filled with Jackson's cock while Jackson filled his mouth with Sarah's pussy.

His hand stilled when he realized the rhythmic thumping on the wall had been joined by a quiet tapping on his door.

Shit. Miss Martha had come by early this morning and probably didn't want to disturb the newlyweds.

"Mr. Nate?" Not Martha, but young Henry Simons. Which meant trouble with the herd or one of the horses.

He dragged his pants up over his hips. His goddamned erection didn't want to be bound behind fabric, but he jammed it into his long-johns and buttoned the placket, ignoring the discomfort. Served him right.

He opened the door a little more forcefully than he'd intended. "What?"

To his credit, Henry didn't jump back or cower. "Bobby Lee Culpepper says there's trouble up at Taylor's Creek."

The farthest edge of Campbell land. Figured that it wouldn't be something in the closest barn. "What type of trouble?"

Henry scratched his nose. "All's he said was there was trouble, and I was to come get you and tell you to haul your ass out there."

Nate cuffed Henry's ear with a light swat, just enough to get the boy's attention. "I know your grandma told you not to use that type of language. You don't use it in front of Miss Martha, you don't use it here."

"You and Jackson curse all the time. 'Sides, Gram ain't around to hear me."

"Miss Sarah lives here now, so I don't want to hear any more language like that." He stepped back in the room long enough to grab his vest before following Henry down the hall to the front door.

"Bobby Lee said I was to fetch Mister Jackson too." The color in Henry's other ear changed until it matched the pink flush of the one Nate had cuffed. "I tried knocking on his door before I tried yours, but he and Miss Sarah was...busy."

Nate grunted. Yeah, Jackson and Miss Sarah had been busy a lot lately.

"He ain't gonna get mad at me for interrupting him makin' babies with Miss Sarah, is he?"

Even with the door closed, the kid had figured out what they were doing? He'd been a few years older than Henry before he'd figured out what those sounds meant. What the hell had Henry seen, or heard, to educate him about procreating?

Shit. Why had that not even crossed his mind? Sarah might already be carrying Jackson's child.

He stopped so fast Henry skidded into his back. The idea of her belly rounded with a babe, her breasts heavy with milk did nothing to ease his desires. If anything, he got hornier than a bull in a pasture full of cows. How sick was that?

He was pulling on his oilskin when Jackson appeared at the top of the stairs, a linen towel pulled around his hips, his hair slick against his forehead. "Trouble?"

"Sounds like." He stared at his buttons, pretending they took all his attention. It was better than seeing the sweat glistening on Jackson's nearly naked body, or the bulge against the thin linen towel, proof of Jackson's ability to satisfy Sarah the way he'd once satisfied Nate.

"Bobby Lee Culpepper says there's trouble at Taylor's Creek, Mr. Jackson," Henry piped up. "He says you're to get down there right away."

"Be right there."

Nate grabbed his hat from the hook and jammed it on his head. He was halfway to the barn where a group of his hands were already saddling up before he realized Henry was racing at his heels.

"Go get your breakfast, son. You've delivered your message."

The boy was halfway across the field when Nate remembered his earlier speculations.

The idea of Sarah having to haul water and do all that heavy work if she were breeding sure didn't sit well. The woman deserved some help. Not that she'd ever complain, but she'd been little more than a slave before she'd married Jackson, and he'd be damned if he wanted her to feel like a servant in her own home. Damn Jackson for not taking care of his wife and making her load easier.

"Henry, ask your grandma to stop by, will you? And you stick around too. See if Miss Sarah needs any help with her chores. Weed the garden or somethin'."

He nodded to the men, who called to him as he headed inside the barn to find Annabelle. She was bridled and her saddle blanket was already in place by the time Jackson stomped into the barn.

"Cold out this mornin'."

"Yup." Jackson was probably all nicely warmed, thanks to his early morning baby-making session. He sure looked mellow as he headed toward Thunder's stall.

"Any idea what the trouble is?"

"Nope."

If anyone had a stopwatch, they might have noticed that he made record time saddling Annabelle. The farm hands might also have noticed that he didn't bother waiting for Jackson before he hauled himself up in the stirrups and rode out of the barn.

Jackson could catch up later. Or not.

He turned Annabelle to the north and spurred her across the fields toward the creek. What type of trouble were they facing? Bobby Lee wouldn't have sounded an alarm for a cow that was having trouble birthing, or who had gotten stuck in a bog. He would have taken care of it himself. So what would have been bad enough for him to send for help? Fire would be the worst threat at the moment. The fall had been so dry the possibility of wildfires had been a constant topic of discussion amongst both the farmhands and the neighboring ranchers.

He scanned the horizon but saw no sign of smoke, which

meant they were probably safe. Rustlers most likely. They'd hit the Barnett place last week, and the Panola spread the week before. Since the creek was at the farthest end of his property, it was a likely spot for rustlers to hit.

When the turf of the fields changed to the loose gravel at the bottom of the hills, he slowed Annabelle down and let her pick her way along the path. He and Annabelle were almost at the crest of the second ridge when he heard Jackson curse. As much as he wanted to pretend he wasn't concerned, he couldn't stop himself from looking back. The wind had caught Jackson's hat. The Stetson was bucketing down the hill with Jackson in pursuit, like a coyote chasing a hare.

Chuckling, Nate urged Annabelle up the final few feet to the crest of the hill and down the other side.

The path was steep; at points there were sheer drops. If Annabelle took a single wrong step, the shale would crumble around them, and they'd plunge down the hillside into the gorge. He reined her in and let her carefully pick her way. He'd gotten a third of the way down when a cougar darted from behind a boulder. He clamped on to the mare's back with his knees, holding his seat when she spooked.

"Fuck!" He wound his fingers through her mane and hung on for dear life, the whole time urging the mare to calm down before they both ended up at the bottom of the gulley.

The shale shifted, and Annabelle's feet slid from underneath her. Before he could kick himself free of the stirrups, the world tilted, and they began a slow tumble down the jagged rocks of the gorge.

SARAH WANDERED INTO THE KITCHEN, HER footsteps echoing through the empty rooms. It wasn't the first time she'd been alone, but for some odd reason, she felt acutely aware of both Jackson's and Nate's absence.

She set to work by dusting every level surface in the house. When they still hadn't returned by the time she'd finished dusting, she set to work polishing the floors. The living room floor shone when there was a knock on the front door seconds before it opened.

"Sarah? Are you here?" Martha walked into the hall, wearing the black taffeta bustle gown she reserved for church. "We missed you at services this morning."

Shoot. "I completely lost track of what day it is."

It was only a half-lie. She'd remembered right before Jackson had rolled her onto her stomach and made her forget her own name, let alone the day of the week. But even if she'd remembered, she wasn't sure she would have attended without Jackson or Nate by her side. While some ladies had welcomed her, others hadn't. Nate had teased her that it was because she'd taken Jackson off the market.

She might have believed him if one woman hadn't waylaid her one Sunday, catching her when Jackson was talking with some of the men. The woman had told her in no uncertain terms that a half-breed like her wasn't good enough to mix with the proper folk of Barnett Springs.

Martha took off her cloak and hung it on the hook beside Jackson's oilskin then handed her a carpet bag. "I was cleaning out my wardrobe yesterday and decided I didn't need all this. I wondered if you'd like any of it."

"Thank you." Sarah opened the bag and poked through it. She pulled out a pair of kid gloves almost exactly the same as the ones she'd admired at the market and examined them.

"These look like they've never been worn. Are you sure you want to part with them?"

"My daughter sent them to me as a birthday present. I didn't have the heart to tell her they don't fit." Martha turned her hands over and examined her fingers. "My knuckles are swelling too much from my arthritis, I reckon. You can go through the rest of it later and if you don't like something, I'll take 'em back."

Martha fixed her with a stern look. "Oh, and don't forget I saw what you had in your saddlebags when you arrived, so don't let your pride get in the way of accepting my cast-offs."

"Thank you. That was very thoughtful."

"It didn't cost me nothin'. Just doin' a friend a good turn, that's all. The boys back yet?"

"No." She clutched the bag to her chest as she trailed Martha into the kitchen. "Do you know what's going on?"

"Only that Bobby Lee came racing into our yard this morning yelling about a cut fence at Taylor Creek and ordering Henry to fetch Nate and Jackson."

A cut fence, not a trampled one. Rustlers, but probably long gone if this Bobby Lee hadn't spotted them. Her legs wobbled despite her relief, so Sarah lowered herself to the bench at the table.

Martha picked up the kettle and filled it from the bucket Sarah kept by the stove. "You were worried about them."

It wasn't a question. "Yes."

"Good." Martha nodded once in approval before she took the kettle to the stove. "To be honest, I'm glad to see you are. When you told me you'd been forced to marry Jackson, I thought perhaps you didn't care for him. That you wouldn't worry about him the way he needs to be worried about. You were so shy and quiet when you first arrived, and he needs a strong woman who doesn't need to cling to him all the time. I didn't think you two would suit."

Despite Jackson's attentions in the bedroom, she'd often worried about that herself. "Have you known Jackson long?"

"Since he was born. His mama and daddy used to own a farm a few miles away from our place. Then after his mama died, his daddy came to work for the Campbells, so Jackson came with him." The kettle on the stove to heat, Martha joined her at the kitchen table.

"So his father was a ranch hand?"

"Lars was sort of a jack-of-all-trades. He helped out with distributing the hay, doing odd jobs, repairing any leatherwork, mucking out the barns. Nothing that required him to be on horseback."

Sarah blinked. "Jackson's father didn't ride?"

Martha's earthy chuckle filled the kitchen. "Oh, heavens no. Lars Kellar was downright afraid of horses."

"Jackson's so at home in the saddle, I assumed he was taught by his father."

"Oh, Lars talked a good game when he arrived in town, bless his heart. You'd think he'd been riding all his life, according to his stories. Of course, that lie was soon disproved. Apart from not being able to ride, he was uncoordinated as all get-out. He couldn't lasso a tree stump to save his life, and the man would clean faint to the ground at the first sight of blood when they castrated the calves."

Which wouldn't earn him a lot of respect from hardly anyone, man or woman. She'd seen that happen to a lot of the newcomers from out east. They all had big dreams of creating a legacy, of taming the land and coming out a land baron. Until they discovered how much hard work, sweat and sometimes just plain good luck was involved in making a ranch successful.

"But Lars was a good man. He treated Jackson and his mama right."

"Jackson's never spoken about his mother." With a father named Lars, Jackson must have gotten his Indian blood from her side. "What was she like?"

Was she like me? She slipped her hand into her pocket and sought the turquoise hatband she'd retrieved from its hiding spot and now carried like a talisman.

"Ruth was a lovely girl. Full of mischief when she was little." Martha took a deep breath, blinking rapidly before she turned away. "She was stubborn, just like Jackson, bless her heart. Headstrong. She wore the pants in that family. She had to because she knew more about ranching than her husband. Even so, Lars worshipped her."

"It didn't bother him that she was part Indian?"

"No, honey. It wasn't her fault who her daddy was, and Lars didn't care one way or another. He was head-over-heels in love with Ruth."

"Not all men are so understanding."

"No, the good Lord knows they're not." She squeezed Sarah's hand again before standing up.

Sarah had to wait until the coffee had been brewed and poured before Martha continued. "When Ruth died giving birth to Jackson's sister...well, Lars pretty much gave up his dreams of his own ranch at that point. Mr. Campbell had a big heart and he knew Lars didn't have enough money to put food on the table for Jackson, so he offered Lars a job. Turned out the one thing Lars was good at was cooking, so he'd man one of the chuck wagons during the cattle drives. From what I gather, there wasn't a man amongst them who wasn't happy when Lars Kellar rang the dinner bell. He taught Jackson to cook too. He was a fair hand at it too. He makes the best omelette I've ever tasted, as well as griddle cakes so light they practically fly off the skillet. " She leaned in conspiratorially. "But don't drink his coffee. I swear it could melt a hole in a plate glass window."

"How old was Jackson when Lars died?"

"He'd just had his twelfth birthday. He was tryin' hard to be a man, but it's tough at that age."

"What happened?"

"They were on a cattle drive. Something spooked the herd, and they started a stampede. Lars was badly crushed when the steers turned over his wagon then ran right over it. He might have survived the broken bones, but he got an infection. It took the poor man over two weeks to die." Martha frowned at her own cup of coffee. "Maybe that's why Jackson doesn't cook anymore. Because it brings back too many memories for him."

The two women fell silent as they sipped their coffee, aware of the wind howling through the trees outside.

Outside, Jackson shouted for her with an urgency that had her putting her cup down with a thump. They hurried to the front porch as a half dozen horses rode into the yard, Jackson's gelding pulling a travois with a still figure lying on it.

"Martha, get your doctorin' kit ready. Nate's been hurt real bad." Jackson called. He pulled up Thunder and swung out of the saddle as the other men gathered around him. They worked with little speech, unhooking the litter from its traces. Jackson grabbed the poles by Nate's head and Martha's son Charles grabbed the bottom. Together they lifted it, carrying their burden onto the porch in total silence.

Sarah held open the door and let them pass, using the opportunity to quickly assess Nate's wounds. They bound sticks on either side of his left leg to act as splints. A rip in the fabric and the dark stain on his thigh told her the skin had been punctured, most likely by bone. Though she knew head wounds bled more than most, she dug her fingernails into her palm at the blood matting his chestnut hair and coating his face. She trailed them into the bedroom, where Martha pulled back the covers on Nate's bed.

The two men lifted Nate as carefully as they might a child and set him on the mattress. Nate was almost as white as the sheets, and more frightening to Sarah, unmoving.

Martha fussed over him, but wasted no time in setting Sarah's shears to his shirt, choosing to cut it from him rather than hurt Nate more by moving him. Sarah chose linens from the trunk at the edge of Nate's bed and set some clean ones aside to use as bandages. She hurried to the kitchen, where she filled a bowl with the water they'd heated earlier. After a second's thought, she filled the kettle again and set it to boil as well.

When she returned, Jackson was talking to Martha, his words clipped and tight. "I think we got his leg set all right, but I think he's got some busted ribs too." He hadn't taken his eyes off Nate. His body was rigid, except for his fists which were clenching and unclenching. She knew that he'd freely change places with his friend, probably even blamed himself for whatever had happened. "I'm real worried about that wound on his head."

Martha touched Jackson's arm, a soothing gesture Sarah could tell did nothing to ease his tension. "Has he come around at all since it happened?"

His lips compressed so tight they were white, Jackson shook his head.

Martha had stripped Nate down, though she'd draped a towel over his groin to preserve his modesty. Blood slowly dripped from the gash on his thigh, though whether it had just started again from them moving Nate or had never stopped she couldn't tell. Bruises and welts covered the rest of his body like he'd been punched by a giant's fist. Only his face escaped unscathed.

If she hadn't seen his injuries, Sarah might have sworn he was simply sleeping, he looked so peaceful.

She touched Jackson's hand, surprised when he laced his fingers with hers in an iron-tight grip. "What happened?"

When he met her gaze, the look on his face was both vicious and bleak. "He'd ridden on ahead and was over the ridge, so I didn't see. All I can figure is that Annabelle lost her footing. They were down at the bottom of the ridge by the time I got to him. She landed on top of him and..." He gestured helplessly to the bed. "They were on pure rock. There weren't nothing soft in that gulley to cushion him."

With a fifteen-hundred pound horse on top of him, it was a wonder Nate was alive at all. Even if he woke up, his wounds could still fester, and his leg might have to be chopped off, and then he'd have to survive that too. Or he could be crippled if his leg didn't set right. Either way, he might never be able to ride a horse again, which he'd probably see as a fate worse than death.

"Shouldn't we send for a doctor?" Sarah asked quietly.

"We've already done so, but Mama here is as good as Doc Shaw," Charles said from the doorway, where he and the other two hands stood watching.

"Miss Martha learned some tricks from her time with the Indians. Shaman magic," another hand murmured.

"No, it's not magic, Russ." Martha shook her head. "Most of my knowledge comes from sixty years of dealing with tragedies like this."

"He ain't dead, so it ain't a tragedy," Jackson growled. "Not yet."

By the time Doc Shaw arrived, Nate's wounds had been

cleaned and poultices applied. The doctor poked and prodded using his bare fingers, then stitched up the wound and declared Nate in God's hands. Just like when her mother had lost control of the buckboard and was injured. At least Nate would be surrounded by friends and family. By love.

Martha shooed her son and the other hands out of the house and sat in the chair beside Nate's bed. Jackson stood guard on the opposite side, though he refused to sit down.

Worried she was intruding, Sarah busied herself by making coffee and greeting the crowd of friends and neighbors, who assembled in the front yard as the news of Nate's accident spread. The kitchen table practically groaned from the plates, casseroles and jars of preserves brought by the wives, while the men divvied up the chores that had to be done. Sarah shut out the more graphic descriptions of other injuries some had faced, taking heart in the tale of the survivors while attempting to ignore those predicting Nate's death.

The mantel clock had long since struck the last chime of midnight before Sarah settled into a chair in the parlor. She'd lost track of time before Martha roused her. "Sarah? Nate's awake."

Sarah closed her eyes and uttered a prayer of thanks. "Does that mean he'll live?"

"Only the good Lord above knows when any of us will be called to His side." Martha picked her way across the dark room and held her hand out. "Go sit with them. It's not just Nate who needs you right now. I can't say I've ever seen Jackson so shook up. I tried to get him to lie down, but the stubborn man refuses. Maybe he'll listen to you."

CHAPTER 7

"I'm right here, Nate." Jackson slid his hand into Nate's limp one and squeezed.

"Hurts."

The pain and weakness in Nate's voice shattered Jackson's composure. "I know, but it means you're alive." *Thank God.* "Doc Shaw wants us to keep you awake for a while before we give you any laudanum."

Nate grimaced, though whether from pain or at having to stay awake unmedicated, Jackson wasn't sure.

"What happened, Nate? Belle lose her footing?"

"Cougar. Spooked her. She okay?"

Jackson shook his head. "She broke her leg real bad." He'd hated racking that bullet into his gun. The mare had been a good little filly, real responsive. Until she'd damned near killed her owner fighting to get up despite the fracture. A cougar would explain her panic. Still, he couldn't have saved her, not with the way the bone had shattered.

"Hard to breathe."

He debated minimizing the damage, but realized Nate

already knew from the pain he was in how bad it was. "Doc Shaw figures you busted at least six ribs." And bruised at least that number front and back. "Bet you got a whopper of a headache too. You've got the biggest damned goose egg I've ever seen." With a possible busted skull, for all they knew.

"Leg...how bad?"

"You busted your thigh bone pretty damned good. Came out clear through your skin. Both the bones in your lower leg too."

The sound and feeling of bone grating on bone when he'd reset it would stay in his memories for the rest of his life. Though the doc had said he'd done a good job setting it, they both knew the break hadn't been clean, and Nate's ability to walk without a limp was still questionable.

Jackson struggled to draw a breath against the lump growing in his throat. "We cleaned it as best we could before we moved you, and Sarah and Miss Martha cleaned it again once we got you back home."

Nate made a half-hearted effort at a grimace. "If it festers..." He dragged in a breath then groaned as his ribs reminded him of the impossibility of that feat. "Remember...your promise."

He tightened his grip on Nate's hand. "I remember."

If it came to that, would he be able to follow through on handing Nate a pistol with a bullet in the chamber? Or have the strength to hold it against Nate's temple and help him fire, if it got to that point? Promises made at age twelve were different when faced with the reality of doing the deed.

Nate's whole body relaxed at Jackson's response. His glance flitted to the doorway, and his lips lifted in the weakest excuse for a smile Jackson had ever seen, though he knew it had probably taken almost all of Nate's energy to manage. He didn't have to look over his shoulder to know who had just walked into the room. Nate never smiled like that at Martha. Or any other woman.

Jackson stared at their still-joined hands. Sarah knew about them already so there was no need to let go. "Look who woke up, Sarah."

"I see." She glided into the room and rested her hand on Jackson's shoulder, her thumb stroking over his shoulder blade. For such a simple gesture, it damned near undid Jackson almost as much as Nate's smile had. Not many people in his life had had his back. Except maybe Martha. And Nate.

And now Sarah.

He reached up with his free hand and covered hers. "Doc says he should be kept awake as long as possible."

"Not what Martha said," Nate rasped. "Trust Martha more."

"I think for now we'll listen to the doc." Sarah squeezed Jackson's shoulder one last time before walking to the far side of the bed. She stroked Nate's hair off his forehead in an unsubtle attempt to check his temperature. "You gave us all quite a scare."

"Sorry."

"Don't do it again, you hear?" Her smile wasn't much stronger than Nate's so when her gaze lifted to meet Jackson's, its intensity startled him. "I don't think either of us could take losing you."

She pulled up the chair Martha had used and settled into it. The two of them sat with Nate, keeping him awake until the night sky changed from indigo to slate grey. Sarah's eyes drooped then closed for longer and longer moments. They'd been closed a good ten minutes by the time Martha glided back into the room.

"I'll sit with him. You take your wife and get some sleep."

He opened his mouth to argue but closed it. Nate was sleeping finally, and there wasn't much more he could do. Unwilling to disturb Sarah, but not wanting her to sleep in that damned uncomfortable ladderback chair, Jackson slid his hand beneath her knees and lifted her.

"Call me if there's any change," he whispered to Martha then carried his wife into their bedroom. When he laid Sarah down on the counterpane, she snuggled into the pillows with a murmur of contentment but didn't wake.

He eased her shoes from her feet, taking the opportunity to run his palm up her calves. Despite his exhaustion, his cock twitched like a damned randy youngster facing his first bedmate. He couldn't explain when it had happened, or why, but it was suddenly important that he hold her skin-to-skin.

It took him some maneuvering, but he managed to get her bodice, skirts and petticoat off without waking her. His attempt to remove her undergarments defeated his efforts, and Sarah awoke with a murmured complaint about his fumbling attempts to undo her chemise.

"Sorry, I was tryin' not to wake you," he admitted. "But I want to get this damned thing off you. So you'll sleep better."

Smiling at his obvious lie, she rolled up on her elbows as graceful as a cat. With her smaller fingers, she picked at the knot that he'd snarled in the laces. When she finally freed them, he pulled the damned thing off her and tossed it on the floor. Her drawers quickly followed. He shucked his own clothes and left them piled in a heap beside hers.

As soon as he slid beneath the covers, Sarah pulled them back. "What's the matter?"

"I'm just checking to make sure you're all right." She met his gaze, her brows drawn together. "I never thought to ask if you were hurt at all."

"Don't you think I would have said something?"

"No. I don't."

He couldn't stop himself from grinning, which damned near drained the last of his energy. "Been with me a month and already you know me that well, do you?"

She nestled her head on his shoulder and rested her hand on his chest in a gesture he found both erotic and comforting. As if she were both claiming him and soothing him all at the same time.

Her ten-minute nap in Nate's room must have rekindled her energies, because her hand smoothed over his belly until her fingers tangled in the hair at his groin. His cock proved it existed separate from the rest of his body because it stiffened and arched as if seeking her hand. Her fingers closed around the swollen shaft and gently stroked him. There was no damned way he was going to sleep now that particular part of his anatomy had awoken.

He shifted, pulling her on top of him. "Your turn to ride tonight, but I warn you, I'm not going to last long."

Her breasts tickled his chest as she leaned over to touch her lips to his. The movement slid his cock through the moist folds, drawing a groan from him. "Don't worry, you pleasured me this morning, remember?"

Had it only been that morning they'd made love?

When he'd been interrupted from taking his own pleasure by Henry's untimely knock. Damn it, he shouldn't be thinking carnal thoughts when Nate lay in the next room, his life hanging by a thread as thin as spider's silk.

"Hey, don't think about it," she whispered. "He'll be all right."

He opened his eyes and found her watching him, her dark

eyes filled with concern. "You even know what I'm thinking now, huh?" "Am I wrong?" He shook his head.

She slid his cock through her folds until the head glistened with her juices. Then she positioned herself above him and took him within her body in a long, slow glide.

As he'd predicted, it took her less than a half-dozen pumps of her hips before he spilled into her.

"Damn, I'm sorry." He flung his arm over his eyes, despair and embarrassment filling him.

"Don't be," she whispered. She pressed a kiss to his cheek before rolling off him and pulled the sheet over them both. "Get some sleep. I'll be right here."

He let himself drift, but he swore right before he fell asleep that she whispered she loved him.

When he awoke, he found find himself spooning Sarah, his cock stiff against her behind in its usual morning salute.

She must have sensed he was awake because she asked, "What promise did you make Nate?"

His erection couldn't have deflated faster if she'd stuck a hat pin in his balls.

"Jackson?" She squirmed in his arms, turning until she faced him. "Last night, you and Nate—"

"I know what you mean." He rolled to sit on the side of the bed, jamming his elbows into his knees. On the other side of the wall, less than ten feet away, Nate lay injured. Vulnerable to something he didn't know how to fight.

"Jackson?" Sarah knelt behind him, resting her head on his back, her arms wrapped around his waist.

He stared hard at the thick plank separating him from Nate. "I gotta go check on him."

Sarah gasped at the angry red streaks extending from beneath the bandage on Nate's thigh. She looked at Martha, seeing the same despair on the other woman's face that she felt. "It wasn't this bad when I changed the bandage this morning."

"We'll clean the wound again. See if we can nip it before it gets worse." Martha removed her sleeves and tucked them into her belt. "Go into the kitchen and make up a new poultice, will you?"

By the time she returned, Martha had stripped Nate down and was placing cool cloths on his neck and chest.

Two hours later, Sarah's back ached from leaning over Nate, wringing the cloths out in cool water and replacing them. When she checked his forehead, he was hotter than he'd been before.

"Don't leave me," Nate called, his voice anxious.

"I won't. I'm right here. So's Martha." She wiped her coolest strip of fabric over his forehead and down his neck.

His head followed the cloth and he sighed when she spread it over his chest. "You've always known..." His words trailed off.

She removed the warm cloth from his belly. When she replaced it with a fresh one, the side of her hand touched his groin.

"God, Jack...been so hard..." Oh dear, he was so fevered he didn't know it was her with him. "So hard having you in the next room...listening to you and Sarah fuck...Wish it was me."

Was he jealous of her taking his place in Jackson's bed? Had he been nice to her to cover his envy?

Was this how Josiah had felt every time he looked at his wife? Did he wonder whether her mama fantasized about Sarah's father? The way she occasionally wondered if Jackson still wanted Nate?

Something had passed between them in the kitchen the

other night but she'd tried to explain it away, tried to pretend she'd misinterpreted it. What if she hadn't?

"Oh, Nate. You'll find someone who will make you happy the way Jackson's made me."

She bent down and pressed a light kiss to Nate's forehead. Beneath her lips, his skin was as hot as a boiling kettle. If he recovered—*once* he recovered, she revised, she'd set out to find him someone worthy.

She straightened when the front door creaked open. Jackson must have come home. She smoothed her apron and took a deep breath, releasing it slowly. He'd had enough to deal with. The demands of the ranch hadn't stopped with Nate's injury. With Nate unavailable, the management fell completely on Jackson's shoulders. Some of the hands used Nate's absence as an opportunity to show their displeasure about taking orders from a half-breed. From the state of Jackson's knuckles at dinner, and the bruises she'd uncovered later the night before, at least one incident had been settled by fistfight.

As she'd expected, he headed straight for Nate's bedroom. He stayed in the doorway, the aroma of cattle and field clinging to him. His eyes narrowed when they fell on the cloth she held, and the one on

Nate's forehead. "He's got a fever?"

She nodded. "It came on this morning."

He took a step into the room then hesitated, glancing down at his clothes and cursed. "Has Martha seen him?"

Sarah nodded again. "She recleaned the wound and put a fresh poultice on it to draw any infection she can." Now it was just a matter of waiting. And praying. "I'm so sorry, Jackson. But he's young and strong. He'll pull through."

He had to.

His hands curled into fists and he closed his eyes briefly. "I want to sit with him, but I've gotta clean up first. Will you stay with him until I get back?"

"Of course." But he'd already disappeared into their bedroom without waiting for her response.

Sarah dipped the cloth into the cool water in the bucket and wrung it out, replacing the already heated one on Nate's forehead. "You have to get better, Nate," she whispered. "You've got people who love and need you here."

Because if he didn't, he might be a specter in her marriage for the rest of her life.

Yet if anyone was an intruder in the relationship, it wasn't Nate. It was her.

Sarah woke to an empty bed for the second morning in a row. She quickly washed and dressed and hurried to Nate's room, where Jackson had kept vigil.

Martha stood in the doorway, a breakfast tray in her hands. She shook her head. "Jackson won't eat, the stubborn man."

"He barely touched his dinner last night too." Sarah peeked in the room and found him sitting on the edge of the bed, wiping Nate's forehead with a damp cloth. "I've never known two men to be such good friends. Mr. McLeod didn't even sit with my mother when she was dying."

Then again, maybe he'd been happy to see the end of the woman who had brought him such shame.

"Come on, Nate. You gotta fight this." The tenderness in his voice brought tears to Sarah's eyes. Especially when he leaned over the still figure on the bed, putting his mouth next to Nate's ear. "You can't leave me. Don't die on me, you hear?"

She could barely hear Nate's rasped response. "You've got Sarah now. You won't be alone."

"Damn it, you can't die. I love you."

Sarah had to step back and rest her head against the hall

wall, fighting the tears burning tracks down her cheeks. How she'd long to hear him say those words to her. If he could love Nate, maybe one day he'd come to love her too. Or was it even possible for a man who loved his friend *that way* to love a woman?

"Jackson can't help the way he feels about Nate, Sarah," Martha said quietly. "They're *Mexoga*, it's part of who they are. Just like Jackson's grandfather. But it doesn't mean he can't love you too."

"*Mexoga?*" Sarah scrubbed at her cheeks.

"Twin-spirited. That's what the Omahas called them." Martha juggled the tray. "Come into the kitchen and have your breakfast before we start the laundry. No sense everyone standing around here."

Sarah trailed Martha into the kitchen as she pondered the older woman's words. Maybe she'd slept too deeply, or maybe her emotions were too jumbled up inside to understand the older woman.

"You said Jackson was like his grandfather. Tell me about him." *Tell me that my husband is capable of loving me.*

Martha hesitated then nodded. "Jackson's grandmother was already living with the tribe when I joined them. Two Buffalo and Standing Horse loved each other like Nate and Jackson. I know our people say it's evil, but it was wonderful to watch how they cared for each other." She got a faraway look in her eye. "Anyway, from what I've heard, Mary fell sick one winter. Two Buffalo was the tribe's shaman, so they took her to him. While Two Buffalo was caring for Mary, he fell in love with her. When she was better, he asked her to stay with them both. They took her as their wife. They both loved her and she loved them equally."

"How do you know they loved her?" All her insecurities

bubbled to the surface. Maybe she was a convenient way to hide what they were. A façade to present to society, should any questions about them be raised.

"Oh, they loved her. I never doubted it."

"Then why did she leave them? Or did they leave her?"

"They didn't have a choice. The settlers were pushing into the territory, forcing the Indians onto reservations. The tribe was forced to hand over anyone with white blood to the soldiers who were clearing the land." Martha's voice cracked. "Mary wanted to stay, but the tribe felt threatened. She had no choice but to leave."

"So they never got to see their daughter."

"They never even knew she was expecting. And Mary had no way of getting them word when Ruth was born."

Rather like her father probably never knew she existed.

"The soldiers handed us to a group of missionaries, who arranged for us to find husbands—things were different back then. There were more men than women, so unattached women were prized. But for Mary...well, when her husband discovered she was expecting a savage's child, he dumped her at the local whorehouse."

It didn't surprise Sarah. Hadn't Jed Hasley suggested exactly that fate for her?

"By that time, I was married to Mr. Simons. When I heard that Mary had died giving birth, God bless him, he let me bring her baby daughter to Barnett Springs. He wouldn't let Ruth live with us though. I found her a good family with an older couple who wanted a child and didn't seem to care that her father was an Indian." Martha clasped her hands on the table and stared at them, frowning. "They treated her more like a servant than a daughter most times, but it was better than her livin' in a whorehouse, where she would have been expected to earn her keep in a much different way."

"Did she know about her father? Her real one, I mean."

"She used to ask when she was a little girl. And again when she was expecting Jackson. I never told her about their arrangement. Just that her father would have loved her. And they would have." Her eyes misted over. "They were honorable men. Strong. Capable. Just like Jackson and Nate."

"That's why you've not said anything."

Martha nodded. "Yes. Now you must not breathe a word to anyone. Not if you value their lives."

CHAPTER 8

Between his busted leg and the aftereffects of the fever, Nate felt as helpless as a newborn kitten. In his whole life, he couldn't remember being confined to a bed for longer than a day. Yet here he was, a grown man reduced to having to ask a woman to bring him his meals and fetch and carry anything else he required. Nate pulled himself up on the pillows. If he could get up and walk out of the room, he would. It wasn't the doc's orders keeping him in the bed, but the fear Jackson had put into him of overburdening Sarah if he fell.

But that left him trapped in this damned room, watching the hands going about their business in the yard. He should be out there, helping them. Instead he was sitting here on his ass in what had once been the parlor but was now a makeshift sick room, forced to endure the parade of well-wishing neighbors.

It was bad enough he was forced to use a goddamned chamber pot, but it was fucking embarrassing to have to call upon Sarah or Martha to help him sit up to use the damned thing. Though neither of them had questioned his request,

Jackson hadn't spared his laughter at his confession he couldn't take a piss unless he had at least one foot flat on the ground.

His anger didn't dissipate until he heard Sarah's soft footsteps in the hallway. She stopped in his doorway, her tongue caught between her lips as she balanced his lunch tray. "Are you hungry?"

"I sure am. If you'll join me." He squirmed back up on the pillows. Damn it, how had he managed to slide down this far again?

"All right." She set the tray across his lap and sat down in the chair beside his bed. "If you eat it all, I have a surprise for you afterward."

While he ate, they talked of decisions that had to be made about the ranch. She didn't always agree with his decisions, but he'd learned in the past weeks that when she didn't, he did well to listen to her well-thought-out arguments. While he'd learned she hadn't had much book-learning, she understood the needs of a ranch, and its hands.

More than anything he liked her innate dignity, accepting his decisions even when they didn't agree. The times he changed his mind to her way of thinking were more telling. Where some people might have not let him forget it, she smiled, nodded and moved on to the next topic.

Damn, Jackson was a lucky man to have found her as a wife. Irritated at the thought, he put down his utensils. "There, I'm done."

Sarah raised an eyebrow but picked up the tray and left without another word. Moments later he heard a strange sound rumbling in the hall.

"Ready for your surprise?" Sarah called from the hall, sounding way too cheerful for his present state of mind.

"Unless it's a new leg that'll let me get up off my as—behind, no."

"Maybe I should have Mr. Evans take this back then." Sarah appeared in the doorway with a wheelchair that reminded him once again of his new status as resident cripple.

"I ain't usin' that thing."

Her lips pursed and she tilted her head. "Very well. If you like staying in that bed all day with nothing to do and no one to talk to, that's up to you." She strode across the floor and grabbed the chamber pot from the shelf beside his bed, placing it on the top of the dresser as far from him as it could be without taking it out of the room. "If you need to use this, you'll have to crawl over and get it yourself or wait until I'm done with the laundry."

Which meant he'd have to hold it until noon. Or later.

Considering his bladder was already whining at the idea of the damned pot being across the room, that might be tougher than it sounded.

He narrowed his eyes at her. "You planned this, didn't you?"

"Borrowing the chair? You know Jackson arranged it a couple days ago. He told you about it at dinner last night." Which they'd eaten in his room as usual in their attempt to keep him company.

"No, I mean blackmailing me. You gave me a big glass of apple cider with my breakfast this morning, twice the size of what you normally bring. And let's not forget those three cups of coffee you've poured for me already. You've planned this."

"It's not good for you to lie in bed all day feeling sorry for yourself. At the very least you'll get bedsores. Besides, the fresh air will do you good. It's a beautiful day today."

"It's not like I can go out walkin' now, is it?"

"No, but you can sit on the porch while I'm doing the laundry."

"What the hell am I gonna do while I'm sitting watching you work?" Blast the devil, he sounded like a petulant child, but she didn't have a clue what it was like for a man to be so helpless, so reliant on others. There were chores to be done, animals to care for. He hadn't missed how Jackson fell asleep over his dinner most nights. Or how the bedroom next door resounded from Jackson's snores, and not from the rhythmic thumping he'd grown used to hearing.

"How about keeping me company?" Sarah said quietly. "With Miss Martha off visiting her daughter, you're the only person I have to talk to during the day."

Her straightforward request accentuated how different she was from Eliza, who would have whined to get her way. It wasn't as if it was a great chore to watch her. She was wearing one of the dresses she'd made from the fabric she'd purchased when he'd taken her to town. Forget all the bows and geegaws adorning Eliza's dress, Sarah's plain gown was understated elegance. Or maybe it was the woman wearing it that brought the elegance to the gown. He tried to picture Eliza waiting on him the way Sarah did, and failed.

"Nate?" she asked.

Besides, if he had to stare at the ceiling for one hour more, he'd be ready to be committed to an asylum. "Sorry. Let's get me in this contraption then."

She stood beside the bed, sliding an arm around him as he attempted to straighten. He couldn't stop his groan when her breast pressed into his side.

"Are you in pain?" She'd turned her head to ask the question, leaving her mouth inches away from his. All he had to do was stretch over and close the gap. Touch his lips to hers. Taste her.

Damn it, damn it, damn it!

"No." *Liar.* This case of blue balls he'd been fighting was gonna kill him as surely as any infection. "I hate havin' to rely on a woman to get me into a goddamned chair." *I want to roll you onto my bed and get you beneath me.* He closed his eyes, reminding himself she was Jackson's wife, not some whore at the local saloon. But damn it, she smelled so sweet, and it had been so long since he'd had any sort of relief in that area.

He was panting and exhausted by the time she wrestled him into the chair, but he was upright and felt halfway human for the first time in a coon's age. "Have the Rangers been around at all with news on those rustlers?"

"You'd have to talk to Jackson about that."

There was something in her tone, a hardness bordering on bitterness. "What's going on between you two, Sarah? Did you have a fight?"

"It's not important."

"The hell it ain't." He couldn't stop the anger welling inside him. His fingers clamped around the arms of the chair. "Jackson loves you, Sarah. And I thought you loved him."

She waited until she'd pushed him over the threshold and onto the porch before she answered. Once she'd set the brakes, leaving him in the shade, she leaned against the railing. "He loves you too, Nate. And you love him."

He'd wondered when she'd get around to that particular subject, Martha having given him a heads up weeks before. The only thing he found surprising was how long it had taken for her to voice her concerns about Jackson's and his unnatural relationship.

You love him. She'd said it as a statement, not a question, her voice holding no sense of betrayal nor the hurt she might be feeling. He struggled to find an answer that would be honest. One that would not deny the truth of her words, or belittle the fears she must have.

"You know he's been faithful to you since you two have been married. You have no reason to question his fidelity."

"I know." She twisted her fingers together. "I love him, Nate. So it's difficult knowing he'll never love me the same way."

If he'd been capable, he'd have gotten out of the damned chair and held her. Comforted her. Shook some sense into her. "Jackson loves you too, Sarah. He's not a man of many words. He's more a man who lets his actions speak for him. I can't think of another woman he's ever brought flowers."

That example caused the tips of her lips to quirk up for a second. Unfortunately, the smile quickly disappeared. "I never meant to come between you two that night."

"We both know that. Jackson doesn't blame you any more than I do. You may have saved our lives in ways you will never imagine."

"Then why hasn't he touched me since you had your accident?"

He barely heard her whispered question, but her anguish was clear. "It's calving season, Sarah. He's plumb tuckered out."

"You're right. I'm being selfish, aren't I?" Her spine straight, she left him on the porch as she set to her chores. Everything she did was done with a quiet determination and dignity.

While neither Jackson nor he had set out to find a wife, Jackson had lucked out. Sarah was the type of woman any man would be proud to have by his side.

Ever since they'd had news that Missy Parker's dress had caught fire while she was doing the laundry, Jackson had insisted Sarah not wear her crinoline when she was doing the laundry or tending the stove, a fashion Nate heartily approved. But as he watched her, he realized he'd have to rethink the wisdom because when Sarah bent down to the basket of wet clothes at her feet, the fabric pulled tight, accentuating every curve and crevice of her ass. Nate's cock stiffened again, leaving him decidedly uncomfortable. It didn't ease a whit when she reached up to hang one of his nightshirts on the clothesline, the sun slipped from behind the cloud, and turned her calico skirts near transparent.

There was no way in hell he'd be able to wear that nightshirt without thinking about her washing it. Hell in a handbasket, now he'd have a hard-on every damned night.

"WHAT'LL HAPPEN TO THEM, CARL?" HOW WAS Jackson going to tell Sarah that her brother had been arrested?

Or that her stepfather had gone missing? There was a slim possibility she might want to head back there, but there was no damned way he could leave the ranch, not with Nate housebound.

Giving Jackson a curious look, the Ranger struck his match on the sole of his boot. He took his time lighting his cigar, waiting until he'd blown out a long stream of smoke before he answered. "They're bein' held until the circuit judge arrives—that's a week Monday. But I have to say, it don't look good for either McLeod or Hasley. Last rustlers facing the judge had their necks stretched, and those fellows had only rustled twelve cattle."

"What about Josiah McLeod? Where's he at?" Jackson scrubbed his hand over his face, not caring that the dirt would mix with the sweat. If he was lucky, it would keep the swarms of mosquitoes away until he could get home. If he never heard another whine of one of those bloodsuckers he'd be happy.

"He wasn't on the ranch when we found the cattle. We tracked him to a local whorehouse, but he was gone by the time we arrived. We're keeping an eye on his place to see if he shows up. If he does, he'll be sharin' the cell with his son. Thing is, we may have to ask your wife to swear out a statement as to what she heard them discussing."

"She won't have to testify in person?"

Carl frowned. "Probably not, but it depends upon if they hire a lawyer."

"But the cattle were found on McLeod's property."

"Not exactly. They were on government land adjoining his ranch. Someone had put up barbed wire around it to keep the herd contained, but as I said, we can't prove Josiah had any knowledge of it since it's at the far end, and it looked like the fencing was fairly new."

"So it's possible he'd claim he hadn't ridden out that way lately and didn't know it existed," Jackson finished.

"You've got the right of it. Either way, we caught Walt red-handed, so he'll soon be dancin' at the end of a rope. As for Hasley, he's claiming innocence. But since we caught him changing the brands, we've got the goods on him so I figure he'll swing too."

Jackson rubbed the back of his neck. "Considering how they treated Sarah, I can't say I'm upset at their end." Of course, it might be different for Sarah but he doubted it. "What about our own troubles? You get a lead on who stole Nate's cattle yet?"

The trouble Bobby Lee Culpepper had summoned them about had turned out to be a cut fence and fifty missing cattle. If Hasley and McLeod hadn't already been locked up, he might have suspected them.

"Nope." With a curse, Carl slapped a mosquito on his arm then took another drag on his cigar. "We've stepped up our patrol of the area, and our guys are keeping an eye out for strangers or cattle whose brands may have been tampered with, but I wouldn't hold out much hope that you'll get 'em back."

"I guess that's as much as I can ask." But damn it, he hated having to leave it in others' hands, even if those people were Rangers as capable as Carl Barnett and his men. Besides, the cattle had probably long since been slaughtered and served up as some easterner's dinner.

"Yup. The good Lord knows we don't need any more vigilantes and their lynchin' parties. In the meantime, you should get home and get some sleep. You look like you're ready to drop out of the saddle."

He must look rougher than he thought. Truth be told, he was having a bucketload of problems keeping his eyes open. "Had some coyotes attacking the herd. Between them and the branding and castrating..."

"Yup. Another reason I prefer to be a ranger instead of a rancher." A cloud of Carl's cigar smoke looped and swirled around his head before it dissipated. "How's Nate doin' these days?"

"Better. He's out of the damned wheelchair and up on a pair of crutches, but the doc ain't sure his leg's ever gonna be as strong as it was before."

"At least he still has it. That's somethin' anyway." The

Ranger slowed his horse as they approached the road to town. "I'll let you know if we hear anything more. Either about the rustlers or your wife's folks."

Carl turned his horse, leaving Jackson to continue toward the Circle Star. He didn't remember closing his eyes until he realized Thunder had stopped walking and had to open them. Damn it if he wasn't in the yard by the barn. Scout, his favorite sheepdog, had already settled down on the porch in his favorite spot.

Shit, he really must have been tired to have fallen asleep on the horse for those last two miles.

Where the hell were the Simons boys? Why couldn't they have been here waiting to take his horse? All he wanted was a hot meal and a soft bed. Was that too much to ask?

He slid out of the saddle with a groan and led Thunder to the barn. His arms felt like lead weights when he lifted the saddle from the gelding's back. He gave his horse a quick rub down and tossed some oats in the bucket and eyed the water. "That'll have to do you for now, boy. I'll send someone in to make sure you're looked after proper later."

With a pat to the gelding's rump, he staggered out of the barn and headed to the house. He'd not even opened the screen door when the scent of cinnamon and apple wafted from the hallway. Perfect, Sarah was making another of her apple crumbles. He wrestled off his boots and followed the delicious aroma to the kitchen.

His hand was on the door when Nate's voice reached him.

"You have magic hands, Sarah." Nate groaned, a deep rumble rich in contentment and...satisfaction? "Yeah, right there, that's the spot. That feels so good."

The last time he'd heard that pitch to Nate's voice had been when they'd been... No. Sarah wouldn't be doing that to Nate.

Would she? Had they been having an affair right under his nose?

Sarah's "You're as hard as a rock" had him shoving open the door and stomping into the kitchen only to have to pull up. Nate sat in a chair while Sarah stood behind him. Massaging his shoulders.

"Hey, Jackson." Nate closed his eyes as Sarah dug her fingers into his shoulder. "Darn it, woman, you've got strong thumbs."

Sarah smiled at him, a completely innocent smile that told him how glad she was he was home. Well, shit. If that didn't make him the biggest horse's ass around.

"I kept your dinner warm." She patted Nate's shoulder then moved to the stove. As she passed him, she reached up on her toes and gave him a kiss. "Why don't you get washed up and out of those clothes? By the time you get back, I'll have it all set out for you."

Washed and changed. He looked down at his hands and saw the dirt on them, compared them to Nate's clean hands. Cow shit and dried blood from the steers he'd castrated clung to his pants, while Nate looked like he was ready to go to church.

What the hell was he doing here?

He grabbed the pail of water she kept warm on the stove and carried it to the bedroom. With a curse at himself, he slipped his suspenders off his shoulders and undid the buttons, not caring that he was a bit rough on them. He should care, though. If he tore one, Sarah would be the one who would have to sew it back on.

Damn it, he wasn't cut out to be a husband.

A slow thumping up the stairs warned him that Nate was headed his way.

It pained him to watch Nate limp into the bedroom. Nate used to be agile. Strong. Vibrant. Now he had to rely on that damned set of crutches Doc Shaw set him up with. It wasn't fucking right.

"Nothing was going on between us, Jack."

He turned his back on Nate, concentrating on pouring water from the pail into the ewer. "Don't know what you're talking about."

"Don't try to bullshit me. You thought Sarah was cheating on you with me when you walked into the kitchen. I saw it in your face."

Jackson braced his arms on the table and hung his head. "When I was coming down the hall, you sounded just like you did when I...when we..." *fucked*. Except it hadn't been fucking with Sarah. Or with Nate for that matter. "I couldn't figure out if I was angry at her for being with you, or angry at you for being with her."

"She's your wife. You have a right to be protective of her. There's no shame to that." Nate leaned against the door. "What's going on between you two, Jack?"

"Don't know what you mean."

"You've been damned ornery lately."

"I've had a lot on my mind, that's all." *You. Sarah. Running the damned ranch. Finding the rustlers. Calving. Castrating. Coyotes.* "Not to mention I'm damned tired."

"Too tired to trust your wife? You think I can't see that you two hardly talk lately, let alone that you two ain't makin' that bed of yours squeak anymore?"

"I'm workin' my ass off trying to keep this ranch together, damn it."

"Yeah, and I appreciate everything you're doin' for me, but you should be payin' more attention to your wife, Jack.

You're drivin' her away. Makin' her feel unappreciated. Women like her deserve a soft word here and there. A wildflower or two by her plate or on her pillow. Like you used to do."

But he'd left one for her just the other...shit. When was the last time he'd brought her a flower? "I don't have a lot of time to mollycoddle her. She knows I love her."

"Does she? You tell her that in words?"

"She knows it."

Nate *hmm*ed. "Sarah thinks you don't love her because you ain't turnin' to her anymore, Jack. She thinks you prefer me and resent her."

"I think you got that backward." He dropped his voice to a whisper. "She knows about us, Nate. She knows what we are. What we've done. She ain't touched me or let me touch her ever since you got sick. Hell, she sleeps as far away from me on the bed as she can."

He missed the gentle touches she used to give him, the passion she'd displayed in their bedroom, the way he'd catch her looking at him—usually his ass—when she thought he wasn't watching. So she still made his chili just the way he liked it, and picked out the pieces of tomato in his salad before she served it to him. That was just her being her. "Can't say as I blame her, I guess. Not many women would respond well to accepting that their husband's a..." He forced the word out, hating to hear it out loud. "...sodomist."

Even though she'd reacted with more grace than he'd dreamed possible, every day he came home wondering if he'd discover she'd moved out. If he'd wake up to a lynch mob.

"So you think she'd be better off with some other fella?" Nate raised an eyebrow in question.

"You know she would be."

"So who should she be with? That Hasley fella back at the McLeod's?"

"No!" Shit, he still had to tell Sarah about her brother's fate. Didn't that make the day fuckin' perfect?

"Junior Turner then. He's single and lookin' for a woman to help him run the mill. She'd have a good life with him."

Jackson sneered. "Turner's twice her age and three times her weight. If he makes it another ten years before he drops from a heart attack, he'll be lucky. Then where would she be?"

"How about Butch Panola?"

"Too short."

"Cooter O'Brien."

Jackson's lip curled into a sneer. "He smells like pig shit even after he's washed."

"How about Nate Campbell?" He thumped across the room, stopping to lift one of his damned sticks to poke at Jackson's chest. "Would I be good enough for her, Jack? A cripple who's forced to rely on others to keep his ranch runnin' smooth?"

Jackson closed his eyes and let his chin fall to his chest to whisper, "You know you would be."

"Even though I've had a man for a lover?"

"It doesn't matter. You're better than me."

"No. I'm not." Nate shifted his weight to one crutch, and let the other drop against the bed. His hand free, he brushed his fingers over Jackson's cheek and cupped his jaw in such a tender gesture it about undid Jackson. "Don't you see? If I deserve a woman like Sarah, then so do you. Why can't you get that through that pigheaded thick skull of yours?"

"Because I love you, too," Jackson whispered. "I know it ain't right that I feel like this for another man when I've got a wife. I've tried to stop, but I can't turn off what I feel for you like I can blow out a candle."

"You can't deny what you are, but you can't punish Sarah for it either."

"I ain't punishing her."

"No? You obviously respect her if you're worried about her like this. And I know you sure as hell enjoy Sarah when the two of you are in bed together."

"Of course."

"Then why the hell haven't I heard the two of you rockin' this old bed since this—" Nate gestured to his leg "—happened?"

"I told you." He stared at the wall over Nate's shoulder. "She's disgusted by me, Nate. She pulls away whenever I touch her. I won't force myself on her."

"You don't have to force yourself. You have to prove it's her you want, not me. Women need to know a man finds them desirable. Hell, you're the one who taught me that." When Jackson didn't answer, Nate shook his head. "What's the matter, Jack? Can't get it up around her? Because I can. Hell, I have a hard-on at least three times a day around her. Do you know how many times I've had to pretend I'm having a nap so I can give myself a hand-job to ease the blue balls I've been getting lately?"

"That's enough." He'd be damned if he'd explain how he'd jerk off watching her sleep, swamped with guilt both for wanting her and for wanting Nate. But hearing that Nate had been thinking of her the same way was too much.

Nate stepped closer, until they were nose to nose. His eyes were narrowed and his lips thinned in the way that Jackson knew meant he was peeved. "Maybe I should go out there and seduce her in front of you. Show her at least one man in this house would enjoy her beneath them."

"The hell you will. Crippled or not, I'll beat you to an inch of your life."

Nate stepped back with a smug look on his face. "Well, it's about fuckin' time."

Jackson blinked. "You don't like Sarah? That was all an act to make me jealous?"

"Aw hell, Jack. Make no mistake, I'd have Sarah in my bed in a heartbeat if I thought I had a chance. But you know I'd never touch her. She's yours. Which is why I figured it was damn well time you realized it."

"Yeah, well, I don't think she feels the same way about me. Besides, it's better for her this way."

"I'm getting real tired of you thinkin' you know what's best for me," Sarah stated from where she stood in the doorway.

Both men turned to face her, Jackson quickly averting his gaze while Nate smiled and held out his hand.

"What is it that you're worried about, Jackson? That I'm going to run screaming into town? Denounce you for loving your best friend?" She advanced on him, skirting Nate, whose grin broadened. "Do you think I despise you? Because I don't. I love you. I worry about you. Both of you."

"Then why have you been turning away from me?"

"The last three times we've—" Her gaze flitted to Nate. Devil take her, she was not going to blush. They'd been discussing her openly, so why should she act like a wilting violet? "—done our marital duty, I've been the one reaching out to you. So I figured it was your turn to take the initiative for once. When you didn't, well, I figured you thought you'd done your duty to me and were wishing you could go back to the way things were."

"You turned me down last time I tried."

"If you'd cared to ask after me, you might have realized I was having my womanly time." Heat bloomed into her face. Did they really need to discuss such a delicate matter in front of an audience? "But that was five weeks ago, Jackson. What's your excuse since?"

Nate positioned his crutches. "You two need privacy so I'm gonna get out of your way, but I expect to hear that old bed creakin' by night's end with you two doin' your *marital duty*, you hear?"

His chuckle faded down the hallway.

Jackson rubbed his forehead the way he did when he had a headache. Between that and the dark circles beneath his eyes, some of Sarah's anger washed away.

"I'm sorry, Sarah. When you turned away, I figured you were disgusted by the thought of someone like me touching you."

"I've never been disgusted with you. I just..." The heat rose in her face again. "I'm still not used to talking about my monthly with you."

"And I ain't used to having to worry about a woman's time, either." He released a long slow sigh. "Can we chalk this up to my pride gettin' in the way as usual? I wouldn't blame you if you don't. It ain't like I'm normal husband material." He ran his fingers through his hair. "Ah, heck, what I'm trying to say is, will you forgive me?"

"If normal husband material is a man like Billy Anderson, whose wife has to hide any money she earns so he can't gamble it away, or like Missy Taylor's husband, who beats her black and blue whenever he gets liquored up, then I think I got the better end of the bargain. And yes, I forgive you."

One side of his mouth quirked up. "I'm not sure that being compared to a deadbeat or a drunk is a compliment."

Sarah wished she could curse as well as Jackson. "I apologize. They were bad examples. Perhaps Miss Martha's husband Abner might be a better one."

"Now there's a cold fish who's never given me the time of day."

She tried to come up with other examples, but for the life of her she knew few other couples as happy as she'd been these last six months. "What I'm trying to say is that you're a good man, Jackson. You've been a good husband and a good friend." She lowered herself beside him and rested her head on his shoulder. "I've never regretted marrying you. And I appreciate how you've been faithful to me even though I wouldn't have been your first choice."

His sigh came from deep down. "And I've never regretted marrying you. I know it's hard for you to understand, but I am capable of loving a woman. Of loving you."

She went still. No one had ever said he loved her before. Was Jackson saying it now? She wondered how she could ask without embarrassing either one of them when she realized his breathing had evened out.

The man had fallen asleep sitting up.

CHAPTER 9

A door slammed downstairs. Jackson opened his eyes and winced at the sunlight streaming across the bed. Sunlight? It had been dusk when he'd come home and made a complete horse's ass of himself. He'd been talking with Nate... no, Nate had left. He'd been talking to Sarah.

He'd apologized. Hadn't he? Had she accepted it?

He turned his head to find her side of the bed empty. Damn it. That it was bright meant he must have fallen asleep and slept the whole night through. A quick check beneath the sheet she'd pulled up over him revealed that she'd managed to undress him, no easy feat because he'd not awoken to help her. That he could remember.

Outside a horse whinnied—Bandit calling to one of the mares, from the sounds of it. Soft footsteps down the hall warned him of Sarah's approach. He frowned when the footsteps went past the bedroom. "Sarah?"

The footsteps stopped and returned. The door creaked open and Sarah, with a basket of folded laundry in her arms, smiled at him. "Good morning. Sleep well?"

"I did. What time is it?" Her soft smile told him she'd accepted his apology. At least something had gone well last night. If he could have just stayed awake and proven how sorry he was.

"It's almost noon."

"Noon!" He shot up, the sheet falling over his hips. "I slept almost sixteen hours?"

"You were exhausted." She set the basket down on the chair and stood in front of him. "Nate and I talked this morning and decided to let you sleep as long as you needed. Nate's asked Bobby Lee to look after things today."

The practical side of him wanted to complain about how she should have gotten him up, but he felt better than he had in a long time. Besides, she looked so pretty standing there. She'd pulled her hair into a bun earlier but it had loosened, and tendrils curled down her neck. The sleep had definitely left his body raring to go.

He rested his hands on Sarah's hips and pulled her between his thighs. He needed her, but he needed to make sure they'd squared things between them. Last thing he could take right now was her walking away.

"I don't quite remember what I said to you last night, but if I didn't apologize, I'm sayin' it now. I'm sorry if I was ignoring you. And..." He swallowed again. "We've not been using your skirts to hide behind, Sarah. Don't get us wrong about that. I love you. I don't ever want you thinking otherwise. "

"I love you too." She stroked her fingers down his cheek and over his jaw. "I'll try to not be embarrassed telling you it's my monthly next time."

"You're not having your monthly now, are you?"

A flush rose up her neck and into her cheeks, accentuating

her golden skin, especially in the bright sunlight that spilled over her. Her chin tucked against her chest, and her eyelids dropped as she shook her head.

"Is Martha here?"

"No." He barely heard her whispered answer.

"Where's Nate?" Not that he particularly cared at the moment. After all, Nate himself had said he wanted to hear the bed creaking. He planned to oblige.

Her gaze shot to the still open door. "He's in his study."

"You got anything on the stove downstairs you need to check on?"

Another tiny shake of her head. Her flush deepened, telling him she knew where his questioning was headed.

"Good." He reached up and undid the top button of her bodice. Then the next. Repeating that she wore too many clothes, he peeled off the layers of bodice and skirt, and all the underlayers she'd donned that morning. Once she stood in front of him without a stitch covering her, he threw back the sheet and stood. His cock jumped as it brushed her belly, reminding him it had been far too long since he'd taken advantage of his husbandly rights.

Jackson pulled the chair in front of the cheval mirror. "Sit down."

She started to head toward the door, but he caught her by the arm. "Where you going?"

"To close the door."

"Leave it. Nate knows where you are and where I am. If he wanders up here, it's his own damned fault."

"But he'll see me..." She gestured down her naked torso. "All of me."

"Yeah, he would." He leaned down and whispered in her

ear. "That's part of the excitement. The danger of being caught in the act. Now sit your ass down in the chair."

Sarah gave him a bemused look but sat. He grinned at how demure she appeared, her hands folded in her lap with her feet crossed at the ankles. While completely naked. He bent to brush a kiss on the top of her head then plucked the pins holding her braids in the bun. Once he'd released her hair from its bonds and it flowed over her shoulders and down her back, he picked up her brush and began to brush the long black strands. "I sure do love your hair."

She sighed but leaned her head into the brush. "I've always wished I had curly blond hair like Missy Barnett's."

He'd not met a woman yet who was happy with their hair —if it was straight they wanted it curly, if it was curly they wished it was straight. But he knew for Sarah, it was more than that. If she'd been blonde, McLeod would have accepted her. Hell, society would have accepted her. More than one man had judged him by the shape of his nose and the color of his hair.

He met her gaze in the mirror. "You're a beautiful woman, Sarah. I'm guessin' anyone who says otherwise is a woman, not a man."

Breaking his gaze, she shook her head. "Not always."

"Then they've got nothing beneath their hats but hair." He set down the brush and cupped her chin with his fingers, lifting it until she met his gaze in the mirror once more. "People who judge you don't know you. And their opinion ain't worth squat. You're a good woman, Sarah. You're a good wife and a good friend."

"You're a good man too, Jackson." She rested her cheek against his belly, her hair whispering over his cock in a silken caress. When she squirmed, he frowned. The room was far from chilly, but he didn't want her to come down with a fever either. "What's the matter? Are you cold?"

"No, sitting here like this. It's...wanton."

Wanton. Good word. And precisely what he needed to ease his tensions.

"There ain't nothing wrong with being wanton with your husband. I like knowin' you're naked just for me." He trickled her hair through his fingers so it curled over her breast. Her nipple beaded into a tight bud with the silken caress. Damn, she was responsive. "Do you know how it excites a man to know his woman will respond to his touch?"

He cupped her other breast and brushed his thumb over the nipple that immediately tightened to match its twin. He didn't miss how her lips parted or her breath hitched. "You're made for a man's pleasure."

Her eyes half-closed, she pushed her breast into his hand and rubbed. She made a soft sound like a cat purring. "Maybe you're made for my pleasure."

Minx. Just when he figured she was shy, she surprised him. "You may be right."

Her hand covered his, pushing his fingers to pinch her nipple. Chuckling, he obliged. "Like that, do you?"

"Mmm." Her eyes closed as she leaned her head against his belly. "I love how strong you are."

She liked him strong. He pulled her nipple and tweaked it harder than she had before. As he'd expected, she groaned in pleasure.

He captured her hand and slid it over her belly until it rested on her mound. "Touch yourself, Sarah. Show me what you like."

It was a game they'd played before. At first she'd been hesitant, but under his tutelage she'd grown confident in pleasuring herself for him. He enjoyed watching her part her folds so he could see her oval opening. Her fingers glistened with her juices, juices that let them slide easier through her dark pink flesh.

"Watch yourself in the mirror while you're doin' it. See what I see."

He paid less attention to what she was doing down there than he did to her reactions, to the way her breath quickened and back arched, to the soft moans signaling she was coming close to release.

"Jackson, please." Her eyes found his in their reflection. "I want you inside me this time."

This time. Which meant she'd been forced to find her own pleasure without him. Nate was right. He'd ignored her for too long.

"How do you want me, darlin'? Do you want to ride me, or do you want me coming from behind?" It hadn't taken him long to discover those were her favorite positions.

"I don't care. I just want you inside me. Filling me. Please."

He lifted her from the chair and arranged the cheval mirror so she'd still be able to watch them. He took her place, then pulled her down to straddle him. "Ride me."

Her glance darted between the image in the mirror and his cock as she positioned her entrance over him. Her head fell back, exposing the long length of neck as she lowered herself onto his length in a slow, torturous slide.

Holy hell, she was so hot, so ready for him. Why the hell had he denied himself this pleasure for so long? He was a damned fool.

They worked together, her undulating over him, taking him deep into her body then lifting until only the sensitive head of his cock remained inside, then engulfing him once more. He played with her breasts, watching her reactions, feeling them in the play of her muscles surrounding his cock.

As she approached her release, he let go of one breast and slipped his hand between her folds and found that sensitive spot. Her body shuddered, so close to release. He pinched her clit, flicked it with his thumb. At first he'd worried that he might hurt her. Other women had objected when he'd touched them like this, but not his Sarah.

"Harder!"

Her half-shouted demand resounded right down to his balls. They drew up tight to his body. She wanted harder, he'd give her harder. He wrapped his arms around her waist and lifted her. He slipped out of her when he stood, so he wasted no time in turning her around and depositing her on her back on the bed.

Her legs fell to either side of his legs, her body open to him, her pussy glistening and swollen as she tilted her hips toward him in invitation.

"Are you sure you want this?" Damn, his voice sounded rough, like he'd been sucking in smoke from a campfire all night.

"Yes." Her breathy response twined with her musky scent, driving his body plumb crazy with need.

"Reach up and grab the headboard, and whatever you do, don't let go."

Her eyes sparkled. "What will happen if I do?"

She thought he was joking? "I'll turn you over and spank your ass until it's rosy red, then I'll fuck it. Hard."

Damned if her whole body didn't shudder in arousal. Dear Lord in heaven, she liked the idea. "Do what I tell you, Sarah."

Still she hesitated. "I'm not sure if I'll be able to hold on, Jackson. I want to touch you too."

"If you do, I'll lose control and this will be over too fast." Because she'd be too sore from him fucking her the way he wanted.

The moment her hands clenched around the wrought iron struts, he widened her thighs with a grip that would probably leave a mark, then slammed his cock into her pussy. They both groaned once he was buried so deep within her his balls hit her ass.

He looked down at the spot where they joined, her so open to him, so vulnerable.

"Jackson." Her hips lifted, pressing him deeper than he thought possible. The hellcat wasn't making a plea, she was making a demand.

Any hesitation he had that she might object vanished. He gave into his wilder side and pistoned his hips. He pounded into her. Again and again and again.

When she thought he couldn't get any deeper, he pressed her knees over her chest, stretching her tender skin over her mound. The crisp hair on his groin rasped across her clit with a wickedly delicious friction.

The bedframe bounced off the walls, and his grunts as he crashed into her faded into the distance. She'd never seen him lose such control, forget to treat her like a china doll. He was all man, hard planes and dark desires. Any doubts she'd had in the past few weeks about his desire for her disappeared like wisps of smoke in a spring twister.

Her body heated, softened, as the head of his cock slid over some part inside her. Her muscles clamped around him, increasing the pressure, her body jerking in time with his pumping. Then his hand snaked between them and touched that special spot between her folds and set off an explosion inside.

When the spasms finally quieted, she let go of the headboard. With a gentle touch, she stroked Jackson's shoulders as he held himself rigid, his cock still firm and pulsing as he spent the last of his seed. His eyes were scrunched closed, a fierce look on his face as if he was in pain. Then all of a sudden he relaxed and slumped on top of her.

"You let go," he choked out. "Bad girl."

Instead of spanking her as he'd promised, he buried his face in the crook of her shoulder and slid his arms beneath her, holding her in a grasp so tight she almost couldn't breathe.

She nuzzled her mouth against his neck, her tongue darting out to taste his salt-tinged skin. Her fingers trailed patterns over his shoulders and down his spine until they reached his behind. She couldn't resist cupping it, squeezing it.

"I'm sorry if I hurt you." He rolled her until she lay spread on top of him.

Her arms planted on either side of his chest, she lifted off of him to shake her head. "No, you didn't hurt me. I enjoyed it. I made you realize that I'm not a china doll."

Maybe that's also partly why he'd not touched her for the past month. Maybe he was afraid he'd hurt her the last time they'd made love?

He dragged the back of one knuckle down her jaw. "Is that what I've been doin'?"

She nodded. "I liked that I can make you lose control like that. It makes me feel...powerful."

"Me telling you to hold on or I'll fuck your ass makes you feel powerful?" He squinted at her, doubt filling his voice.

Put that way, perhaps not, but still she grinned and nodded. "I can't explain why, but yes."

He made a noise in the back of the throat that told her he didn't believe her. Yet he cupped her breast and tweaked the nipple harder than he usually did, sending a streak of heat straight down to her pussy. "You do like it when I'm rougher, don't you?" She nodded again.

"I wonder what else you'd like." He rolled her back beneath him, trapping her. "Would you let me tie you up? Let me do anything I want to you?"

"Tie me up? People do that?" She narrowed her eyes. "Then what would you do?"

He captured her bottom lip between his teeth, tugging on it slightly before he released her. "I'd like to see you on your knees in front of me, your hands tied behind your back and my cock filling your mouth, for starters."

He'd taught her how to take him in her mouth before, but the idea of being tied up, him completely in control of how fast or how deep was both frightening and exciting.

His hand trailed down her side and beneath her to caress her behind. "I want to make your ass mine one day."

She wrinkled her nose. "I don't see why you'd want to do that."

"Just think of it as me stakin' my claim on every inch of you."

She'd never had anyone claim her before. No one had ever wanted to. The idea of him taking her so carnally set off a delicious dark thrill that made her wonder just how much of her mother she had inherited. "So tell me, what do I have to do to stake my claim on you?"

He pulled her over him again, stroking her hair. "Darlin', you've already staked your claim. I'm yours."

His cock hardened between them. Grinning, she squirmed down his body until she was between his thighs. His groan when she touched her lips to his cock reverberated through her, sending off tiny quakes deep within.

After running her tongue around his smooth foreskin, she parted her lips and took him into her mouth. She loved burying her nose in the crisp hair, smelling his musky scent. She loved the taste of his salty essence, the first drops of which leaked from the tip betraying his arousal.

"Fuck yeah."

The first time he'd used the obscenity in front of her, she'd been shocked, but now she knew it meant he was losing control. Maybe she was perverse, but she loved that she had such power.

"Harder, Sarah. Suck me down."

Her hips rocking, she increased the pressure.

Remembering what she'd seen back in the barn, knowing he enjoyed rougher treatment than she'd at first believed acceptable, she wrapped her fingers around the base. From the pressure of her fingers and the suction of her mouth, his hips arched until his cock touched the soft spot at the back of her throat. With her free hand, she reached between her own legs and found the bundle of nerves that was already pulsing in need.

"Oh, fuck, I'm not going to last long."

Relishing the control she had over him, Sarah kept up the pressure and rhythm until his cock swelled against her tongue. Moments later, his harsh shout bounced off the walls, and hot seed splashed over her tongue. As his cock softened in her mouth, she pulled away, cleaning the head of the last drips of his essence.

He pulled her up to rest her head on his shoulder. "I didn't think I had it in me to do that a second time."

"You didn't have it in you," she said with a chuckle. "You had it in me."

"Minx." Keeping her head on his arm, he rolled until he

was facing her and played with her breast, his breath warm on her damp skin.

She rocked her hips against the strong fingers he'd left on her mound. "Would you think poorly of me if I confessed I pictured you doing this to me when I was in bed the night I met you? That I also had fantasized about you?"

"Did you now?" His fingers parted her folds and teased the sensitive nub.

"I pretended I was in that stall with you. Between both of you," she whispered. "And that you were both touching me. At the same time."

His fingers stopped moving. "Would you like that? Having both of us in your bed?"

She pulled back and stared at him. No, he couldn't mean actually inviting Nate into their bed. Could he? Fantasies were all well and good, but what he proposed was licentious. Shameless.

Thrilling.

"Did you know Nate listens to us at night?" His fingers resumed teasing her clit.

"Such a pity he had to miss this show then, isn't it? Maybe we can give a special performance one day. If I ever get up the nerve."

He chuckled and dragged her against him in a tight embrace. "I love you, Sarah. I never thought I'd have a wife who could make me laugh the way you do. How did I get so lucky?"

It was a question she could ask herself. Of all the men she might have been forced to marry, she'd have chosen Jackson every time.

CHAPTER 10

Sarah clutched Nate's elbow as they walked into the barn. "Be careful right here. The floor's uneven."

"I am being careful. You don't need to be a mother hen," Nate grumbled, but sweat glistened on his forehead from the effort. It was the farthest he'd ventured since he'd switched from his crutches to a cane. While he was moving better, she worried that he might fall and reinjure himself. Not that he'd listened to any of her arguments, the stubborn man. "Go do whatever it is you need to do."

There was nothing here for her to do. His ranch hands had already swept out all the stalls and laid down fresh bedding. The water troughs were full, the hay bags filled.

He stumped through the barn, wandering down the aisles before he did a wide turn and returned. He didn't speak when he wandered to the pasture, where several of her mares grazed. Knowing him, Nate was contemplating how to convince her to saddle one and let him ride.

"Martha was sayin' old Junior Barnett bought himself one

of those steam-powered tractors. It can cut faster and with less hands than the way we're doing it now."

Would wonders never cease? He wasn't plotting to ride. She walked over and stood beside him, watching a team of horses pull a combine through the hay. The quiet whirr of the machine's wheel as it turned had always comforted her.

"I saw Junior driving it when Jackson and I went to church on Sunday. It was noisy and smelly, and Jackson said they cost a fortune. I can't see most folk giving up their horses for one."

"Maybe. But Martha said Junior was thinking of taking it around and offering to cut other people's fields. If the price was right, it might be worth talking to him. Especially if his claims that they save the number of hands you need are true."

Plodding hoof beats drew her attention away from the fields. Nate followed her gaze as Carl Barnett approached. "Now there's a man who's not happy."

Sarah had to agree. Normally the Ranger rode up to the house at a trot. He'd swing from the saddle, deliver whatever news he had, then leave. Today the horse plodded down the lane at its own pace.

Nate stirred once Carl drew closer. "Maybe you'd better go into the house, Sarah. Let me talk to him."

"No. I want to hear what he has to say. It's probably just that he hasn't caught the rustlers or found your cattle yet." It wasn't as though they could hang her stepbrother twice for his crimes. Unless they'd found Mr. McLeod and charged him as well. It still bothered her that she hadn't mourned Walt, or worried about her stepfather. At least say a prayer for them? By the time she'd followed the thought, Carl had stopped his horse in front of them and had already swung out of the saddle.

The Ranger hurried to Nate to save him the trouble of

walking over the uneven ground. "Afternoon, Mrs. Kellar. Is your husband around?"

"I'm afraid not. He's up in the back fields checkin' on the sorghum."

"Oh." He took off his hat and scratched his head. "Maybe I should come back later. When he's available."

She shook her head, concentrating on the Ranger. At least he'd asked to speak to Jackson first. Otherwise she'd suspect he'd been hurt. Or worse. "It's bad news, isn't it?"

"Yes, ma'am. About the worst it can get. That's why I think it might be better if I speak to your husband first."

"I'm not about to faint or get hysterical on you, Mr. Barnett." When Sarah folded her arms and tapped her foot, the Ranger looked to Nate for help.

Nate sighed. "You might as well tell her whatever news you've come to deliver, Carl. She won't let it go now."

His eyes narrowed, and a muscle in his jaw twitched. He even eyed his horse as if he might leave without telling them anything. To Sarah's relief, he finally heaved a sigh. "We received a tip that after your brother's sentence was carried out, a couple of his neighbors confronted your pa about whether he knew about his son's activities. Or may have even orchestrated them."

"They killed him." She searched herself for any sign of grief, but other than a mild sadness found little.

"Yes, ma'am. They threw his body down the well, which is why we didn't find him for so long." He turned his hat in his hands. "We've given him a Christian burial and all, so you don't need to worry about that, but there remains the matter of the ownership of his ranch. As his daughter, you're his next of kin, which means you inherited his land."

"Oh." Which meant she owned—Jackson owned— a

ranch larger than Nate's. They had a home of their own. A home filled with unpleasant memories that she'd been glad to see disappear into the distance behind her. "I'll have to discuss the matter with my husband."

"Fair enough, ma'am. I can direct you to a good lawyer up around those parts if you need one to see to the paperwork of transferring things over."

"Thank you."

Carl replaced his hat on his head and stared at the mare rolling in the dust. "Well, I should be gettin' along. I'm sure you have a lot to discuss with your husband."

"I suppose congratulations aren't exactly proper." Nate said quietly once the Ranger was out of range. "But I know it'll ease Jackson's mind knowing you two will have a place of your own."

"This place has felt more like home to me than that place ever did." She faced him. "But it's time we moved out, Nate. We've imposed upon you long enough."

"I haven't minded." He rested his weight on his cane, lifting his free hand to brush the back of his knuckle down her cheek. "There's nothing I wouldn't do for you or Jackson."

She touched her fingers to the back of his hand. "You're sweet."

"I'm not sweet. I'm selfish." His voice dropped to a whisper. "I'd give anything to have you both with me for the rest of my life. If you decide to move back home, I'd sell up here just so I could move closer to you."

"We don't have to move far. We can sell the old one and build something respectable around these parts. Maybe we could buy the old Cain place. Then Jackson can still help you run the ranch." Did she dare mention that Jackson had already made inquiries about buying the abandoned farm?

"Even down the road is too far from you both, Sarah." He swallowed. "Don't leave. Please."

JACKSON'S SHIRT CLUNG TO HIM AS HE TRUDGED onto the porch where Sarah sat, her sewing abandoned beside her. "Too hot to even sew, huh?"

"The light's gone, and I don't want to bring out a lantern because it'll attract all the bugs."

She lifted her head when he bent down to kiss her. As their lips touched, he cupped her breast, her nipple peaking beneath the thin cotton gown she wore. In this heat, she'd not only given up wearing her corset the way he'd asked, but her bloomers and chemise as well. The thought of only a single layer of fabric standing between his skin and hers had his cock lengthening.

When she moved to stand he stopped her. "I'm gonna go inside and wash up. You stay out here and enjoy the breeze."

He grabbed the bucket of water she kept handy and washed up in record time. A quick check showed Nate, shirtless, at the desk in his study, poring over the farm accounts. Thank heavens Nate liked that type of thing, because numbers had never been his strong point. Show him a cow having problems giving birth, or ask him the best way to stack hay, that he could handle. Hell, he'd rather be shoved in a stall between a stallion and a mare in heat than face a wiggly column of numbers.

He dashed upstairs and changed into a clean shirt and lighter cotton trousers before returning to the porch.

A glance over the pasture confirmed there were no hands

lingering in the fields, and he couldn't see anyone in the barn. If he couldn't see them, he doubted they could see Sarah sitting in the deep shadows of the porch. But even so, he led her into the kitchen and seated her in the rocking chair she kept by the now cool ashes of the hearth. Once she was in place, he closed the door and locked it, then shuttered the windows.

He held up his suspenders and let them dangle from his fingers. "Remember what we talked about the other night, about me tying you up? And giving Nate a show?"

Her tiny gasp and the way her tongue flicked out to lick her lips gave him all the proof he needed that she knew exactly what he wanted, and would get as much enjoyment from it.

"Stand up and turn around, Sarah."

When she stood to obey him, the fabric over her breasts tightened, highlighting that her nipples had drawn even tighter. He stepped behind her and ground his erection into her ass as he cupped her breast, thumbing the hard buds.

He wrapped the suspenders around her wrist. After a moment's consideration, he slid the rocking chair around so even if a farmhand did happen to wander out of the barn and saw a shadow on the kitchen curtains, they wouldn't be able to see what she was doing.

Confident there'd be no unwanted witnesses, he tossed the pillow she'd been sitting on onto the porch by his feet, then took her place in the rocker. "Get on your knees, Sarah."

Even with her hands tied behind her, she sank to her knees with the grace of a dancer.

"Scootch closer, so you don't have to lean so much." Once she was in position, he unbuttoned the placket of his trousers and drew out his cock. "Suck it down. You know how I like it."

He couldn't stop the groan when her lips closed around the engorged head. She engulfed him in moist warmth, her tongue pressing on all the right places, applying just the right amount of suction to draw his balls up against his body. He wrapped her braid around his fist and held her still, giving himself a chance to regain the control he was so rapidly losing.

Even held in place, her tongue continued to swirl around the head, to flatten along the length of his shaft and press him against the roof of her mouth. The quiet squeak of the kitchen door hinges warned him that Nate had joined them.

The light from the oil lamp glistened off the sweat of Nate's chest, accentuating the delineation of his muscles. Using the crutches then the cane had built up his arms and shoulders until it looked like he could lift a heifer with little strain. The cotton fly of his trousers was drawn tight over his erection, and his gaze was locked on Sarah's mouth.

"We've got company, darlin'," Jackson whispered, though he didn't take his eyes off Nate.

Sarah started and released him with a wet pop. To his surprise, she relaxed when she saw their visitor was Nate.

"Do you like watching me do this to Jackson?" she asked softly.

"Yes." Nate's whispered answer couldn't hide the desire in his voice.

She sat back on her heels and tilted her head up at Jackson. The minx wet her lips, glanced back at Nate then at the cock bobbing in front of her face, and back to Nate again. There was no mistaking the heat in her gaze, or the question in it.

Jackson touched his fingers to her cheek. "Are you sure?"

She nodded. "I am. The choice is yours."

"Nate." Strange how though there was no one else around to hear, they all spoke in whispers, as if they were all afraid to break the moment building between them. "Come over here."

"No, I should...leave."

"Nate." Jackson sharpened his voice. "Get over here. Now."

After a moment's hesitation, Nate padded over to them. To Jackson's surprise, instead of Nate unbuttoning his fly and freeing his erection, he lowered himself to his knees beside Sarah.

"Thank you." Nate touched his lips to Sarah's in a whisper soft kiss, then turned his head and swallowed Jackson's cock down to the root.

"Fuck!" Jackson's hips lifted from the chair that rocked, thumping against the wall. "Holy hell in a handbasket."

His fingers twined through Nate's hair, dragging him away from his now-aching cock. Releasing Nate, Jackson stood up and stepped away from them both, running his hands over his head. "That's not what I meant. Sarah wants to suck you off as well as me, you idiot."

His ire and surprise ebbed when he saw the need on Nate's face. From the heat in Nate's eyes, Jackson knew his friend was also remembering the last time either had dared touch each other. And the long months since. "Aw, shit."

Sarah's admission that she'd been aroused watching them that night pushed itself from where it had been flittering on the edges of his mind to front and center.

"Sarah? Remember what you admitted to me the other night?" Jackson said, careful to keep his voice quiet as he lifted her to her feet and freed her wrists.

"About how you felt watching Nate and I?" She nodded, her eyes searching his.

He let his hand drift to her behind where he squeezed her firm buttock, one of his fingers stroking the tight crevice. "Do you remember me sayin' how I'd like to claim you here?"

She nodded again, her tongue darting out to moisten her lips.

"How about we fulfill both those fantasies tonight?"

Did you know Nate listens to us at night? That as he listens, he indulges in his own fantasies. That he pleasures himself in time to us?

God, Jack...been so hard...you in the next room...listening to you fuck Sarah... Wish it was me.

When she opened her eyes, they were both watching her. Waiting. For her to run screaming into the night perhaps? To condemn them? For what?

If I hadn't seen for myself what he was doing, how you enjoyed how rough he was.... There was no denying she'd been aroused by watching them in the barn. Nor could she have missed the love on Nate's face when he dropped to his knees beside her, or his desire when he'd taken Jackson's cock in his mouth. Instead of being horrified the way she thought she should be, the images that her imagination conjured of the three of them tangled together were provocative. Exciting. Decadent.

"Think about it, Sarah. Two men worried about nothing other than your pleasure. Two mouths to kiss you." Jackson's hand dropped from her jaw to cup her breast where his thumb stroked her nipple until it ached. "Two mouths to suckle these lovely breasts."

He ground his growing erection against her mound. "Two men inside you, filling you."

At the same time? How would that be possible?

As if sensing her confusion, Nate stepped behind her, pressed his erection against her behind. He dipped his head beside her ear, a hint of the brandy he'd been drinking lending an exotic essence to the moment. "Imagine us fulfilling your every pleasure, Sarah. Both of us."

Her breath was hard to draw as they undulated in rhythm against her. Her head fell back against Nate's shoulder, her breasts pressing into Jackson's chest.

Jackson's head dipped, his lips skimming over her cheek. His beard rasped her neck and ear when he captured Nate's mouth. The passion between them as they kissed drove her breath from her.

They were both breathing hard by the time they parted.

"Did that bother you? Watching me kiss Nate?" Jackson's eyes may have been hidden by shadows, but she could hear the anxiety in his voice, knew how important her answer was to him.

"No," she breathed. It had been so right, so perfect.

Jackson held out one hand to her while Nate captured the other. She let them lead her upstairs. Instead of turning into the bedroom she and Jackson shared, they continued down the hall and into Nate's bedroom.

Despite the heat of the room, she shivered as they removed her dress and let it fall to the floor in a heap.

Jackson put a hand out and stroked her cheek. "Are you afraid?"

She looked from one to the other. She wanted this, she wanted them both. "Would you think badly of me if I said I find it exciting?"

He closed his eyes, but not before she saw the relief in them. "You're a remarkable woman, Sarah. I'm lucky to have found you."

"We're both lucky," Nate said quietly. He leaned over and caught Sarah's lips—a hint of Jackson clung to him still. His kiss started out light then grew both in heat and need.

At first Sarah felt awkward. Then Jackson stepped behind her, his hands cupping her breasts and pulling her back against him until she found herself trapped between the two men once again. Beneath her head, Jackson's heart pounded, his erection pressing into the cleft of her behind, telling her he was anything but jealous. Confident in his love, she gave herself over to Nate's bold kiss.

Jackson bent his head forward and kissed her neck. One of his hands released her breast and slipped between her and Nate until he found the juncture of her thighs. His callused fingers parted her folds, stroked her tender flesh, his movement driven by the undulations of Nate's hips against the back of his hand.

The love shared between the three of them flooded her, removed any doubt, sent her spirit soaring. Society be damned, how could she deny the love she had for them, or theirs for her and each other?

One hand resting on Nate's behind, Sarah hooked her left hand behind her head and stroked Jackson's shoulder. The change forced her breasts up. Nate broke off the kiss and dropped to suckle one of her nipples, using teeth and warm tongue to excite the hard bud. Jackson turned her head toward him and captured her mouth, taking Nate's place, his kiss demanding, his breathing harsh. She couldn't stop her moan when Nate dropped to his knees and nuzzled her mound.

Between Jackson's fingers and Nate's tongue, the two men brought her to a state of bliss where only their whispers, their touches and kisses existed. They lay her on the bed, Jackson lowering his head to her breasts, suckling and teasing while Nate lapped her labia. His sideburns and beard grazed the tender inner flesh of her thighs. He dipped a finger, then two into her slit until she writhed beneath him.

Jackson rolled from the bed long enough to ditch his

trousers and shirt. When he returned, he secured her hands over her head and straddled her until his cock bumped against her lips. Her body and hands held in place by Jackson's weight and Nate's hands on her thighs should have left her feeling trapped. Instead, she found it freeing to be able to concentrate only on pleasuring Jackson while receiving pleasure herself.

Her body shaking with need from Nate's caresses, Sarah lifted her head and slid her lips over Jackson's cock, over the fat head and down the shaft. Jackson's groan as she hollowed her cheeks and sucked on his shaft heightened the sensations within her own body. When she'd confessed to Jackson her darkest secrets, she'd never imagined she could be driven to such heights of carnality. That she was even capable of giving, and receiving, such sheer passion.

Unable to contain her orgasm any longer, she bucked against Nate's mouth. A second later, Jackson's cock swelled, hot streams of his seed shooting over the back of her tongue in steady pulses. She swallowed, desperate not to lose a single drop of his salty essence. Her head lifted from the pillow even as he attempted to withdraw his softening cock from her mouth, her tongue lapping the final drops from its head.

Her bones had softened, and her body sank into the soft feather mattress when he moved off her. In a dreamy state, she watched when Jackson turned to Nate and ran his hands over Nate's glistening chest. Jackson didn't take his eyes off her, but his breathing grew ragged and shallow.

Sarah's nipples ached, and her body heated until she was sure she was about to combust when

Jackson's skilled fingers quickly undid the buttons of Nate's fly and freed his erection. She was fascinated at the way Jackson's hand engulfed the heavy shaft. But Nate's eyes widened and he stiffened, his gaze fastened on Sarah.

"Ssssh, relax. Sarah enjoyed watching us in the barn that night. She needs to see us now too." His voice was rough as he positioned himself behind Nate, his chest tight against Nate's back, golden skin against pale contrasting in the candlelight. "Trust me, Nate." "Sarah?" Still Nate resisted.

She licked her lips, still tasting Jackson's seed on them, when he tightened his grip on Nate's cock and stroked from the thick hair at its base to the bulbous tip.

"He's right," she said. "I want to watch."

Reassured, Nate slumped against Jackson's chest. His hand closed over Jackson's, and the two of them quickened their strokes.

"God, I've missed this, Jack." Nate groaned, his eyelids heavy under Jackson's ministrations. The head of his cock glistened as his seed started to leak from the tip. Entranced at the play of emotions over both their faces, Sarah watched, her breathing matching Nate's pants.

"Sarah," Jackson said, holding her in place with his gaze alone. "I want to take Nate while he's in you."

It wasn't a question, yet she knew she held the power to say no. Not that she would have—could have—denied either of them. But there were other considerations. "Aren't you worried I may end up carrying Nate's babe instead of yours?"

A fire flared at the back of his eyes, not of jealousy but of pride. "Not at all."

Nate touched her ankle, the only part he could reach. He stroked the inside flesh with a gentle assurance. "If we did conceive a child tonight, I would cherish and protect him with my dying breath. The same as I would protect you and Jackson."

"But you'd never be able to claim it as yours."

"Not publicly, but any child you bear, mine or Jackson's,

will be loved just as deeply, no matter which of us were the father."

"Sarah?" Jackson said. "It's your choice."

Heavens, it was positively wicked to consider the thought of lying with another man while her husband watched. Even more scandalous was the moisture gathering in her private places as she imagined it. But none of it mattered. "I want to do this."

"Then come here for a moment. I'm going to need your help while I get us both ready."

Not understanding what he needed to do to *get ready*, she rolled to her knees. Jackson curled her fingers around Nate's cock until she learned the rhythm, and strength, he'd been using. While his cock was velvety hard like Jackson's, his length and girth were different and it took a moment to position her hands to both their comfort.

Nate fastened his lips over a spot on her neck beneath her ear, his breath whispering over her skin in an erotic caress, his hips pumping his shaft into her hand. Using his hands and his body, he pressed her backward onto the mattress until he covered her like a blanket, his sex nestling against hers, the hair at his groin softer than Jackson's against her mound.

A drawer opening in the table beside Nate's bed drew Sarah's attention to where Jackson was standing.

He lifted a small jar from the drawer before closing it. Fascinated, she watched as he dipped his fingers into the jar then coated his cock with the oily cream it contained. Still holding the jar, he placed a knee on the mattress and smoothed several fingerfuls of the ointment along the crack of Nate's backside.

Nate groaned when Jackson penetrated his rear entrance with his fingers. "Oh, God, yes."

Against her mound, his cock hardened. A warm drop of his seed landed on her heated skin, rousing Sarah in a way she'd not thought possible.

Sarah lifted her hips, rubbing his cock along her folds, spreading her moisture until sweat dripped from his brow onto her chest. On one pass, the head of his cock slipped into her passage, and his whole body shuddered. He wasn't as thick as Jackson, but he was slightly longer and he touched places deep inside when he slid fully into her.

She let out a gasp when he retreated slightly, the head of his cock rasping against a sensitive spot inside. "There. Right there."

"He's got to hold still for a moment, Sarah," Jackson instructed as he removed his fingers and positioned his cock at the opening. "Nate, relax or this is gonna hurt."

"Do it fast, because I'm not sure I can hold off much longer. Sarah's so fuckin' tight, and what you were doin'...I can't hold back, Jack." Nate's voice was strangled, his eyes scrunched closed as if he were in pain.

Nate's eyes opened wide when Jackson breached his body, then the two men held perfectly still. Though Sarah couldn't see exactly what Jackson was doing, there was no denying the fierce look in his eyes, or the way Nate's cock hardened inside her. No, she realized, it wasn't pain he was in, but ecstasy.

The skin on Nate's hips whitened as Jackson's blunt fingers tightened their grip, and he eased back and began a slow rhythm. Each time he pulled away, Nate pulled back from her. As Jackson pressed back inside Nate's body, Nate pressed into her pussy. In a strange way, Sarah felt as though it were Jackson fucking her instead of Nate. It took a few moments to work out a rhythm, yet they worked in a synchronicity that required no words.

Soon Nate was thrusting deep inside her, driven by Jackson behind him.

She struggled for breath with each stroke, the emotions of the evening, of lying with Nate at the same time as Jackson being forced to the background. The love they had for her and each other was clear. If she could do nothing else, she would return their love in any manner they asked. She concentrated on the sensations they aroused. The differences between Nate's touch and Jackson's. The sounds of the bed's ropes creaking with each stroke, the wet sounds of flesh slapping flesh. The twin sets of deep groans above her. The spicy scent of their passion mingling on her skin.

Soon even those faded as Nate's cock excited the tender tissues of her passage, building into an unbearable pressure that exploded in a mixture of light and heat.

She was barely aware of the pulses of warmth jetting deep inside as Nate followed her over the brink. A breath, maybe two later, and Jackson's bellow joined Nate's.

Astounded by the strength of his orgasm, Jackson pulled out of Nate. Beneath him, Nate sagged over Sarah, whose head lolled to the side, both of them gasping for breath. He touched his lips to Nate's shoulder, then waited until Nate rolled off of her before pressing a light kiss on Sarah's cheek. "Thank you."

Sarah lifted a hand as if it were an effort and threaded her fingers through the hair at the back of his neck. If her touch was gentle, her expression was even softer, her eyes filled with love. "I love you."

Tears prickling, threatening to spill, he closed his eyes and buried his face between her breasts. There was no way he could ever express what tonight meant to him. What a gift her acceptance of his proclivities had been.

He swallowed hard, once, twice, until he regained the control that threatened to flee. "I love you too, Sarah."

His legs were as weak as a newborn calf's as he walked over to the wash basin to clean himself. The possibilities, and the dangers, of what they'd done flooded his conscience. One night, he told himself. Just this one night, and then he'd talk to someone about buying the old Cain place. Because there was no way he could stay so close to Nate without wanting this every night.

After cleaning himself thoroughly, he grabbed a wash cloth, dampened it and returned to the bed. He found himself avoiding Sarah's gaze as he cared for Nate. Would she want him touching her now she knew what he was? Though she'd seen Nate with his fist around his cock, seeing her husband fucking another man's ass should have been enough to send any woman screaming into the night.

Keeping his gaze on Nate's behind, he continued his ministrations. Sarah picked up the jar he'd placed back on the table and opened it. His breath caught in his chest when she sniffed it, then smoothed some between her fingers.

"I like the scent. Is that almond?"

"Yes." Oh, God. With the washcloth scrunched in his fist, he dropped his eyes as soon as his gaze met hers.

Her fingers came into his field of view, rested on top of the back of his hand. "Jackson? Are you afraid I'm ashamed of you? Because I'm not."

She pulled an edge of the washcloth from between his fingers until she'd freed it completely. After she'd tossed it back to the basin, she lifted his hand and pressed her lips against his knuckles in a kiss so tender, his chest ached.

"I love you, Jackson. I will always love you."

He wrapped his arms around her and held her tightly,

burying his face in her hair. "I thought that now that you'd seen...now that you knew..."

"That I'd leave you? No," she whispered. Her fingers smoothed over his back until his muscles relaxed. She drew him down to the bed to lie between both her and Nate. Two sets of hands, one male, one female, skimmed across his chest, two sets of lips caressed his nipples. They teased and comforted, exciting him while at the same time calming him, until he drifted off to sleep to the gentle murmur of their voices.

Jackson awoke, his body curled around Sarah, who still slept. At some point one of them must have turned down the oil lamp, or it had spluttered out during the night because the room was still dark. It took a moment to remember why they were in Nate's bedroom instead of their own.

Then the memory of what they'd done, what they'd shared came flooding back.

Marveling that she'd accepted his desires without demur, he kissed the back of Sarah's head. He'd never understand how he'd managed to get so lucky in finding a wife.

Two seconds later the bedroom door creaked open. The moonlight streaming down the hall outlined Nate's figure in the doorway.

"Where are you going?" He kept his voice low in deference to the still sleeping Sarah.

Nate didn't turn around. "My leg's stiff, and I need to walk around for a bit. Besides, I figured you'd want some privacy."

Considering what they'd done earlier, giving them privacy seemed incongruous, and as much as Nate's comment about his leg rang true there was something else in his tone that bothered Jackson. "Is something wrong, Nate?"

"No." Before Jackson could reply, Nate disappeared down the hall.

"Damn it." He eased from Sarah's side but there was no sign of Nate in the hall. Since he hadn't heard Nate's cane thump down the stairs, and he wasn't in either of the other bedrooms, the only place left that Nate could have gone was onto the second story porch. His hunch was right. The moonlight limned Nate's body in silver where he stood against the railing.

So much for needing to walk off the stiffness.

Nate spun away from him the second his fingers touched Nate's shoulder. He grabbed for the railing before he lost his balance, but his cane fell through the wooden slats and landed on the ground below.

"Don't touch me." Nate held up his hand as a barrier to stop him from touching again. "For pity's sake, just leave me alone."

"Damn it to hell, man. What's wrong?" His chest splitting wide, he forced himself to drop his hand when all he wanted to do was grab Nate and hold him close. "Do you regret tonight?"

Nate closed his eyes. "No. But I should never have agreed. It's going to kill me when you leave."

"Leave? Where am I going?"

"The McLeod place. It's yours now. Yours and Sarah's. Didn't Sarah tell you?"

"No." McLeod was dead? Why hadn't Sarah told him? Because he'd kept her busy in the bedroom—in Nate's bedroom—instead of listening to her.

"They found McLeod. He's dead. Which means since Sarah's technically his next-of-kin, she's inherited his farm.

You've got your own place, Jack." Nate turned around so Jackson couldn't read his face. Not that he needed to. From Nate's slumped shoulders and the way his voice had fractured, Nate was holding on to his dignity with a slim thread that threatened to snap at any moment. "You have no reason to stay here anymore."

His mind raced through the possibilities. They had their own land, their own ranch. He wouldn't have to rely on anyone else ever again. But he did have a reason to stay here. One very important reason. Nate himself.

Had tonight been good-bye without him realizing it? No, he was getting ahead of himself. "Did Sarah say she wanted to go back?"

"No. That's why I was going to the kitchen when I interrupted you two—to find out what you'd decided."

"I hadn't told him yet." Sarah stood in the doorway. She'd put on Nate's robe. A strange warmth floated over him at how they blended together so well. She met Jackson's gaze. "I was going to tell you earlier, but I got *distracted*. Besides, I didn't think it was something we had to decide about right away."

"It's not," Jackson said slowly. "What's your gut saying about it?"

"I don't have any fond memories of that place, and I was glad to leave. The idea of going back..." She walked into Jackson's outstretched arm and snuggled against him. "We could sell it. Maybe buy some land here close by? The old Cain place you were talking about, perhaps? It's close enough that we could have some cattle of our own, and you could still see Nate."

It was a solution he'd considered himself. Part of him clung to her saying he could still see Nate, while another part of his conscience reminded him of his marriage vows. If she decided to leave, he'd go with her. It didn't matter what he felt for Nate —he was Sarah's husband, and he'd given her, and the preacher, his word.

Nate forced his gaze to Sarah and took a deep breath. "There is another solution. You could stay right here. With me. Make this your home permanently. Like we are right now. As lovers."

Lovers. The three of them. Sarah's knees were still wobbly from the orgasm they'd given her earlier. Was it possible to have this type of pleasure night after night? Them pleasuring her and her them?

Maybe loving between men involved a different set of emotions. Maybe they only sought physical pleasure, not emotional.

You can't leave me. Don't die on me, you hear? I couldn't take it. I love you.

Maybe not.

"The choice is yours, Sarah." Jackson stroked her shoulders, then trailed his hands down her sides to cup her breast. "I'll do whatever it takes to make you happy."

"And if I said no, you'd walk away, sacrifice your own happiness?"

"If you're not happy, I wouldn't be either. I told you, I gave you my vows to love and cherish you. If that means leaving here, never seeing Nate again, then I will."

"But you love Nate too. I heard you, when you thought he was going to die." She squared her shoulders. "I can go back to the McLeod place, hire a manager to run it for me, and you can stay here to live with Nate. The way you were before."

"It's true," he said slowly, his words sounding like they wrenched from his soul. "I do love Nate. But that doesn't mean I'm not capable of loving you too." When she shook her head, he gripped her arms until she looked at him. "Does Miss Martha love one of her children more than her others? She loves 'em all equally, Sarah. It's the same with me. I can love Nate at the same time that I love you."

He glanced at Nate who stared out over the dark pastures. "Besides, even if you do pack up and leave, it's too dangerous for us to go on the way we had been. What happened that night in the barn proved it."

"He's right, Sarah." Nate faced them. The moonlight highlighted the stark fear and desperation in his face. "Things around here aren't the same as they were even fifteen years ago. There's more people movin' in, bringing rules and order to these parts that we never had to worry about before. You leave, and people will start talking. And as much as they may have whispered about us, tolerated us even, one day someone's going to get a burr under their saddle, and they'll stretch our necks for us on that old oak out front.

"Same goes." Nate's smile was crooked. "Don't leave me, Sarah. Don't leave Jackson either. We both love you too much."

If she left, they might be happy together for a while, but she wouldn't be. She loved Jackson. Life without him and Nate in it would be cold, dull and lonely. If she left, she'd constantly worry that their secret would be found out, and they'd be lynched. She wouldn't be able to live with the knowledge her presence might have saved their lives.

"I don't want you to wake up and realize you resent having

me in your bed instead of Nate." *I don't want to wake up and discover I'm unwanted. Unwelcome.*

"It doesn't have to be that way," Nate stated.

Before he could continue, she waved him off any arguments. "Because you say it won't? My mother told me Mr. McLeod 'forgave her' for sleeping with my father after I was born, yet he never touched her again. They grew to despise each other."

"Sssh, it's just a suggestion." Jackson tucked her head beneath his chin. "We don't have to make any decisions tonight. Or even this month."

Nate touched her shoulder. "Come back to bed. Both of you. I don't want to waste another minute tonight. Even if we do nothing else but sleep, I want you both beside me."

They followed him back to his bedroom, where they positioned her between them. Perhaps they knew she couldn't sleep, for they distracted her with kisses and gentle soothing touches until the sky was grey with the coming dawn.

CHAPTER 11

After a brief moment of panic when she opened her eyes, Sarah realized she was in Nate's bedroom. Alone in Nate's bed. The memories of what she'd done— they'd done— the night before played through her mind. While she knew it was scandalous, she couldn't find it in herself to regret a single moment.

The delicious scent of bacon drifting up from the kitchen tempted her to climb from the bed. The ewer had been filled with fresh water—Jackson's doing, most likely—but its water was lukewarm, not hot, which meant he'd filled it a while ago. She dunked the wash cloth into the water and washed her face and hands in what her mother would have called a lick and a promise, but it would have to do. She dressed quickly, not bothering to seek her corset from her own bedroom, simply pulling the shift they'd dropped on the floor the night before over her head.

To her surprise, the only person in the kitchen was Martha. Before she could dart back to her bedroom to get properly dressed, the woman looked up from sweeping the floor, her gaze taking in Sarah's unbraided hair, loose dress and bare feet.

"Good morning, Martha. I didn't realize you were back." Reminding herself that Nate had told her this was her home, or might be if she and Jackson decided to take Nate up on his offer, Sarah held her head high. "Have you seen Jackson or Nate this morning?"

"Jackson's already left for the fields, and Nate said he was restless, so he had the boys hook up a carriage and has driven into town." Martha gestured for her to sit at the table then slid a plate of fried potatoes, bacon, sausage and eggs from the oven.

Sarah toyed with her food, cutting the sausage into pieces and moving the eggs around on the plate.

Martha slanted her a glance she couldn't read. "Are you going to eat that sausage, or just play with it for the rest of the mornin'?"

What had happened between them last night was no one's business but their own. But she had so many questions. She wanted a woman's point of view, but that would be impossible. With a sigh, she set her fork down on her plate. "I guess I'm not hungry."

"That can portend a great deal." Her gaze fell to Sarah's flat stomach. "Shall I be offering Jackson my congratulations next time I see him?" Martha's expression hardened. "Or Nate?"

"I beg your pardon?" She flattened her hand over her belly. The idea that she could be carrying either man's child caused the blood to flood her face. Yet if she did get with child, she'd love it no matter its father, and she knew with absolute certainty both men would love the babe as well.

"Did you think to hide that you were sleeping in Nate's bed this morning, not your husband's?"

Her veins chilled to ice as she realized the damage the woman could do in the community. A whisper here and there could quickly set the rural grapevine afire. "I shared the bed with my husband, thank you. And I'll thank you to keep such mean-spirited gossip to yourself."

To her surprise, instead of being angry at the rebuke, Martha nodded. "Good. There's hope for the three of you yet."

"The three of us?" They were that obvious? She forced herself to pick up her fork and stabbed a piece of sausage. "I have no idea what you're talking about."

Martha nodded as she slipped onto the bench opposite Sarah. "I've got eyes in my head, girl. And ears too. Jackson loves you, but so does Nate. And those boys love each other too, as much as they try to deny themselves. Finding you in Nate's bed this morning only confirmed what I've suspected for a while now. You're lying with them both, aren't you? And Jackson approves. Was it his idea? To share you?"

The small amount of food she'd forced down threatened to make another appearance. "You mustn't tell anyone. Please."

Martha reached across and patted Sarah's hand. "I'm good at keeping secrets. Trust me. I'd kill myself before I'd hurt Jackson."

The emphasis the older woman placed on her last sentence spoke volumes. If only Sarah could decipher what she implied. She ran through what Martha had told her earlier about Jackson's grandparents. Of how Mary had lived with two men. How Martha had fought to bring Mary's daughter with them. Of her anger that she might have betrayed Jackson.

Sarah sat up in her chair. Why hadn't she seen it before? "There was no Mary, was there? You're Ruth's mother. It's not Nate you come to visit, it's Jackson."

Martha stared, her eyes wide in horror. "No. You mustn't say such things."

"But I'm right. Aren't I?" She leaned forward, the pieces clicking together like a child's puzzle. "You didn't start working for the Campbells until after Jackson's father died. After Jackson came here to live. *You're* his grandmother."

"You mustn't tell anyone. Not even Jackson." Her fingernails dug into Sarah's wrist, though Sarah doubted Martha was aware how hard she was gripping. "You have to promise me."

"For heaven's sake, why not? Jackson thinks he's alone in the world. Do you know what it would mean to him to know he's not? That his grandmother is alive? You have to tell him. Please, Martha."

"I can't. Abner made me promise I'd never acknowledge Ruth or him as blood kin. I begged him to let me keep her with us, but he refused. To this day, he says it's God's punishment for my fornicating with savages. If he found out anyone else knew, that I'd told you, he'd send me away. I'd end up working as a street walker selling myself to drunkards and worse for pennies."

"Jackson would never let that happen. You could come live with us."

"I couldn't. Abner would tell everyone what I'd done. Neither Jackson or you would escape censure either. Please, you mustn't say anything to Jackson or anyone."

"She doesn't have to tell me because you just did," Jackson said from the doorway.

Martha jumped from her seat, her hands twisting in front of her. "Please forgive me. I loved your mother. I hated having to leave her with the Gallaghers, but I didn't have any choice. Abner was willing to overlook where he'd met me, but if I hadn't agreed to give Ruth up, he would have left me in the whorehouse."

He took off his hat and ran a hand through his hair. "Did Mama know who you were? That you were her real mother?"

"No. I didn't dare tell her." Tears streamed down Martha's cheeks. "I wanted to tell her, please believe me. But when she was little, it was too dangerous, and when she was older, when she was carryin' you, I was too afraid. I had a home and a husband who accepted me. I had Charles and Olivia to think about. While they knew I'd lived with the Indians, they had no idea that I'd been...they have no idea Ruth was their half-sister."

"You don't need to worry. I won't tell anyone." His hand shook as he placed it on her shoulder. "You really are my grandmother?"

"Yes." Hope flared in her eyes, and her voice steadied.

He enveloped Martha in his arms and cradled her, his eyes closed. Sarah pressed the heel of her hand to her chest as they stood there for a long time, just rocking each other. When they finally broke apart, Jackson swiped his thumb beneath his eyes and blew out a long breath. "If Abner ever hurts you or threatens you, if he tries to use it against you because he thinks someone knows, you come to me. You hear? You don't ever need to worry that you won't have a home."

Sniffling, Martha smiled and reached up to touch his cheek. "I'll remember that."

She took a deep breath and straightened her spine, returning to the in-control woman they knew. "Well, I think I've had about all the surprises I can handle for a day. I think I'll leave you two alone." She faced Sarah. "You treat my grandson right. Or you'll be answering to me."

"Yes, ma'am." Sarah smiled at the wink the older woman gave her.

Once they were alone, Jackson tugged her into his arms. "I've known her all my life and never figured that she was my grandmother. How'd you figure it out?"

"Maybe because I haven't known her all my life?" She rested her head against his chest, his heart thumping softly against her ear. Steady. Strong. "You don't blame her for not telling you or your mother, do you?"

He paused so long she wasn't sure he'd answer at all, then he finally shook his head. "She made the best of a bad situation. Despite what Miss Martha thinks, the Gallaghers were kind to Mama. Probably kinder than that horse's hind end Abner Simons would have been to her."

One of the farm hands yelled to another, reminding her that he'd returned unexpectedly. "Why did you come back anyway?"

"I saw Nate leaving in the cart and figured we should talk without him around." His expression grew serious. "About what he proposed last night. The decision is completely yours, Sarah. If you want to go back and see if we can make the McLeod ranch work, I'll go with you. If you want to sell it and buy something closer around here, I'll do that too. Last night... that was a gift I cannot repay. But I took vows to be faithful to you, Sarah. I intend to honor them."

That he was giving her full control touched her. He was willing to walk away from not only Nate, but his family. "If I never set eyes on the McLeod ranch again, I'll be happy. I know how important it is to have family, to have people you care about and who care about you. I'm not about to take Martha away from you now you've just found her."

She looked around the kitchen and realized she'd spent a

lot of hours either working with Martha talking and laughing or sitting at the table with Jackson and Nate, making good memories. By marrying her, Jackson had become her family. Which meant Martha was as well. And, though he might not be related by blood, Nate.

But was their plan fair to Nate. He'd originally planned to marry her so he could have children, heirs. Even if she did bear his child, he could never claim it. She repeated her concerns to Jackson.

"We talked about that already, Nate and I," Jackson said. "He's written up his will so if anything happens to him, we'll inherit the ranch."

"Won't his family try to claim it?" There was no way the courts would side with Jackson or her over Nate's family.

"He has no family left to claim it so it's not an issue," he said softly. He trailed a finger down her cheek. "You don't have to make a decision today, Sarah. We've got lots of time."

Why should she deny herself the happiness that swelled within her by adding distance between them? "There's no decision to make. I think we should stay here. Martha will continue to come over, and no one will question it. With Nate's injury, he's going to need help, and no one will question us staying to help him out either. I may end up in the fires of hell for admitting it, but I loved last night. I love you, and I love Nate too. I say we agree to Nate's suggestion."

His body went absolutely still. The emotions that played across his face—hope, love, need—told her she'd made the right choice. "Are you sure?"

"More than any decision I've ever made before." She laced her fingers with his and led him upstairs.

He stayed still as she untied his bandana and smoothed it out, laying it on the bed. His chaps were soon removed and set aside. Her teeth tugging at her bottom lip, she unbuttoned his shirt.

A gentle smile tilted the corners of his lips, softening his normally hard expression. He pulled his shirttails from his trousers and over his head. His undervest quickly followed it.

When she knelt in front of him and unbuttoned the front placket of his pants, Jackson stroked her hair, lifting the long strands and letting them fall through his fingers. No words were needed between them as he stepped out of his trousers. The flap covering the opening of his drawers was taut, outlining his erection. She traced a finger along the thick shaft, then tugged at the silk tape at his waist.

The wood hard beneath her knees, Sarah lifted her eyes as she let his drawers fall around his ankles. Her tongue darted out to moisten her lips. She touched it to the slit of his cock and swiped it around the head, leaving it glistening. His grip on her hair tightened when her lips closed around the shaft and slowly travelled its length until her nose rested against the nest of curls at its base.

A horse whinnied outside, a stallion calling to a mare perhaps, and a crow called its raucous caw as it flew overhead. But inside their bedroom, all she could hear was the pounding of her pulse in her ears and Jackson's soft growl.

At first he let her set the pace, a gentle back and forth motion, her tongue slapping at his swollen head with each pass. His cock swelled against her tongue, and his fingers held her in place. He pumped his hips, forcing her to relax the back of her mouth with each stroke. A dribble of his seed was all the warning he gave her before he cursed, his hips bucking.

She swallowed, almost frantically, as pulse after pulse of hot salty essence poured down her throat.

As his cock softened in her mouth, she licked it clean then pulled back to sit on her heels.

"Damn. I'd intended to finish inside you." He held out his hand and lifted her to her feet.

"I like doing that for you." From the way her body pulsed deep inside, and the moisture between her thighs, her body approved too.

"I don't recall objecting to it." The lines at the side of his eyes crinkled as he smiled. He swiped his thumb over her lips. "I want to pleasure you too, but it's gonna take me some time to recover."

She ran a finger down his breastbone. "I can think of a couple things you can do in the meantime."

His eyes darkened. "So can I. Starting with getting you as nekkid as the day you were born."

She backed up when he crowded her, stopping only when the back of her knees hit the bed. "Seems fair, considering what you're wearing."

He undid just enough buttons to be able to pull her dress over her head. Once he'd removed it, he dumped it on the floor.

She crooked him a smile. "That poor thing really needs an ironing, the way it's been treated lately."

"I prefer you dressed the way you are now." His fingers trailed down her neck and around her breasts, tracing her areola that puckered at his touch. "I had no idea you weren't wearing a chemise under your dress. If I'd known I'd have had you naked and flat on your back downstairs."

"Promises, promises."

She screeched when he picked her up and tossed her on the mattress. Before she could move, he was on top of her, the bandana in his hands and a feral look in his eyes.

"Grab on to that headboard again, darlin'."

Her body aching in anticipation, she obeyed him without hesitation. Once he'd secured her, he began to tease and titillate every inch of her body, his lips latching on to her nipples as his hands found all those places he knew excited her.

Nate toed off his boots in the front hall. He started to head for the kitchen to see if Sarah was there so he could talk to her about his plan, when he heard a rhythmic squeaking overhead. Instead of the normal guilt-ridden envy, love flooded through him.

Last night, Sarah and Jackson had given him a gift he'd never be able to repay. Themselves and each other. Both had so much to lose by inviting him into their bedroom, yet they'd done it without hesitation.

He debated going back outside and leaving them to complete their marital relations without an audience but instead found himself upstairs and halfway down the hall. He couldn't stop himself from pausing in their doorway and watching.

Was there anything as beautiful as Sarah? Her head thrown back, hands tied to the headboard with a red cloth that Nate recognized as Jackson's favorite bandanna. They were both naked, with Jackson's dark head nestled between her thighs. The muscles rippling along Jackson's back, his butt taut, rocking against the mattress in search of his own release as he pleasured his wife.

Though he couldn't see Jackson's face, Nate knew what he'd see. A look of ecstasy, of sheer animalistic carnality.

The heady scent of sex filled the room. Sarah gasped the unique sound signaling she was about to find her pleasure. Hard. Moments later, her body arched off the mattress, her limbs shaking as her release overcame her.

Not for the first time, he wished he was an artist who could capture their expressions, the sheer love they had for each other, for eternity. But he doubted anyone had that type of talent, not even if they had one of those newfangled cameras.

Jackson raised his head, his cheeks and lips glistening with Sarah's juices. "Go get that jar of ointment from your bedroom, will you, Nate?"

Not even a hello. Obviously Jackson had known he was watching.

Nate chuckled to himself as he did as Jackson bid. He handed the jar to Jackson. He already knew Jackson didn't intend to use it on him. "Mind if I watch?"

"You're gonna do more than watch. Get your clothes off and get on the bed." Jackson's voice was rough, guttural, which Nate knew meant he was primed and ready and having a hard time holding off not burying himself in Sarah and fucking her brains out.

Nate quickly stripped off his clothes and knelt on the bed beside Sarah. "What do you have planned?"

"Lie down beside her. You'll find out soon enough." Jackson untied Sarah's hands and chafed her wrists. "Turn over, darlin'."

A questioning look on her face, she lay belly down, her face turned toward Nate. She reached out and stroked his hip with her fingers as Jackson nudged her thighs apart and positioned himself between them.

As Jackson liberally coated his fingers with the ointment, Nate remembered the night before, when Jackson had coated him the same way. He couldn't contain his surprise when Jackson reached over and smoothed the ointment over Nate's erect shaft.

"I want you to be inside Sarah at the same time as me," Jackson said, his voice getting even rougher.

He dipped his fingers in the jar again and smeared a large dollop along Sarah's crevice. He worked one finger into her rosette. He stopped when it was knuckle-deep. "Try not to tense up. Just breathe in and out, nice and slow. It'll go easier that way."

Sarah's eyes had closed, and her lips were pressed together. After a moment, her body relaxed, and the whiteness of her lips changed back to pink. The hand that had stopped stroking his hip resumed its motion, the softness of her fingers so different from Jackson's rougher caresses. That she trusted them both was a testament to Jackson, and a gift to him.

"This will be Sarah's first time having a man take her here." Jackson met his gaze. "So you'll need to go real slow when you enter her."

Nate closed his eyes in an attempt to hide the emotion swamping him. That Jackson would trust him to initiate Sarah —his wife—to such an intimate invasion was a gift beyond imagination.

Jackson stretched out between them, the heat of his skin a brand where it touched Nate. "Come up here, Sarah. You're going to be riding me tonight."

Sarah's smile lit the room. She straddled Jackson, her skin glowing gold in the warmth of the late evening sun. If Nate could paint, he would have wished for a brush and canvas to capture the beauty of the two of them joining at that moment, the love filling Sarah's face, the passion in Jackson's. If he was a poet, he would have written sonnets about the scent of love filling the air, or the rugged beauty of Jackson's muscles as he held Sarah above him, the thickness of his thighs, the crinkly nest of dark hair at his groin mingling with Sarah's softer thatch. A musician would have composed sonnets in an attempt to immortalize the soft moan Sarah made when she lowered herself over Jackson's hard shaft and took him completely into her body.

Instead, all he could do was watch in awe, and silently thank whatever had brought them both into his life. Whatever had convinced them to let him share in this moment.

"Hey, Nate? You just gonna sit there watchin', or are you gonna scoot in behind and join us?" Jackson's voice had lowered at least an octave, the roughness revealing that he was equally affected.

Nate shook himself from his reverie and nodded. He rose to his knees and captured Sarah's lips with his own. She tasted of honey and Jackson. He knew he'd remember that flavor for the rest of his life. They were both breathing hard when he broke off the kiss. "Now give that big guy a kiss for me, will you?"

She nodded, but he didn't miss the tightening of her muscles, or the way she licked her lips.

"I won't do anything that hurts you," he said. "I promise."

"I know." Her gentle acceptance as she leaned over Jackson started a shake in Nate's hands. Had he ever been handed such a precious gift?

"Help her relax, Jack. I'll try to go easy on her. Sarah? If it starts to hurt, just let me know."

"She'll be fine." Jackson plundered Sarah's mouth, murmuring soft words to keep her relaxed. His hands played with her breasts, his fingers plucking her nipples to hard peaks the way that he knew aroused her.

Nate positioned himself at Sarah's entrance. Sweat dripped off his forehead by the time he'd sheathed his entire length in her tight canal. When Jackson's cock slid along Sarah's thin membrane separating them, his whole body shook.

He closed his eyes and lost himself in the rhythm, relishing the feel of Jackson's cock rubbing up against his as they worked out a rhythm of thrusting within their mutual love. The crisp hair of Jackson's thighs rasped against the back of his thighs every time he withdrew from Sarah. When he thrust back within her, the soft satin of her behind cushioned his belly. Their mixed pants and groans quickened, and Sarah's body convulsed around him. Unable to hold off his own release, he poured into her.

As he slumped over them both, he suddenly realized they'd never given him an answer. Or was this it?

Did this mean...had they decided to leave? Or to stay? Was this a welcome to the rest of their life together? Or was this their way of saying good-bye? He opened his eyes to find Jackson watching him. Whatever they'd decided, he would take the gift Jackson offered and treasure it for the rest of his life.

Jackson swallowed against the emotion flooding Nate's face. Though Nate cut off his view by burying his face in the crook of Sarah's shoulder, there was no mistaking the half-choked breath, or the way his shoulders tightened as he held her tight.

Unsure how to show his own emotions, Jackson leaned over Sarah and caught Nate's mouth with his own. Nate seized on the kiss with an almost desperate intensity, thrusting his tongue into Jackson's mouth. He tasted of Scotch, the good stuff, better than he could afford at the saloon. Cigar smoke clung to his skin. The scents reminded him he could be rougher with Nate, let his wilder side free. There was something empowering about not having to worry about Nate getting hurt, so he took command of the kiss.

"Please," Nate whispered. "Tell me what you've decided. Was this your way of sayin' good bye?"

Jackson couldn't stop the laughter from bubbling up.

Wrapping Sarah in his arms to keep her close, he rolled onto his side, sending Nate sprawling across the bed. "You know, for so smart a man, you sure are plain dumb sometimes. Ain't it clear what's goin' on here?"

"Hush up." Sarah prodded him in the stomach, jolting his breath from him. "It's not funny."

"It is funny," he grumbled, rubbing his abdomen.

"We're staying, of course." Sarah rolled on her back and covered the hand Nate had placed on her belly with her own. "We both love you, Nate, and Jackson belongs here, with you. With his family. And now you're my family too."

Jackson reached across and placed his hand over theirs. "Our family."

EPILOGUE

CIRCLE STAR RANCH

A little girl's shriek of joy rang clear across the pasture and floated into the kitchen. A deep unmistakable chuckle joined the laughter. Unable to resist the temptation, Sarah left off kneading the biscuit dough, wiped her hands, and headed to the corral. She slowed when she saw Jackson leaning against the fence with one foot on the bottom rail. In the distance, two of their grandsons raced their horses against their fathers. Their whooping and hollering carried over the recently mown fields in a song of sheer pleasure she wouldn't trade for anything. But Jackson's eyes were on Nate riding his latest acquisition, a gelding named Lightning, his arm carefully wrapped around their granddaughter, Ruth.

"She's going to be a natural rider, that one." Pride filled Jackson's voice.

"Just like her granddaddy."

His hands gnarled with age, Jackson slipped his arms around Sarah's waist. She rested against him as they watched the duo trot a slow circuit around the corral. It wasn't just pride for their granddaughter Jackson felt, Sarah knew. Despite the doctor's gloomy predictions he'd never ride again, Nate had wrestled his way back into the saddle less than a year after his accident. Though his hair was now completely grey, he sat as strong and proud as he had when she'd met him.

Her father's turquoise and silver band glinted from Nate's hat, a gift she'd given him the day they'd made their decision to enter into their unusual relationship.

"Lookit me, Gammy, I'm riding with Pawpaw Nate," Ruth called when she noticed Sarah watching them. Sarah's heart did a leap at the joy in Ruth's small face with its pointed chin, tiny replicas of Nate's eyes twinkling back at her.

"So I see, darlin'."

"I swear, that girl's got Uncle Nate wrapped around her finger. She's already been riding once today." Alice, Ruth's mother and Sarah's daughter-in-law, took her place at the split rail fence beside them. "How'd she manage to talk him into taking her up with him again?"

"All she had to do was ask," Jackson said without taking his eyes off the pair. "There's nothing Nate wouldn't do for our children."

Our children. *Their* children. Sarah wondered if Alice realized that her husband was actually Nate's child, and Ruth his granddaughter. Not that he'd treated any of their children, or grandchildren, any differently—he loved them all equally.

"She'll be wanting to gallop all by herself next, I wager," Alice continued. "I swear that child isn't afraid of anything."

"You can blame her grandma's influence for that." Jackson's smile shone bright beneath the shadow cast by his hat. "I ain't never known Sarah to back away from a challenge. Seems like all our young'uns inherited her backbone."

To punctuate his point, the Kellar grandsons raced into the barnyard, closely followed by their fathers. Though each loudly claimed victory from their race, Sarah suspected her sons had let her grandsons win. One day in the not-too-distant future, Jackson could tell them, they'd be hard-pressed to win against their strapping sons.

As her boys, young and old, led their horses into the stable, their daughter appeared on the porch, one hand carefully holding her swollen belly and her soon-to-be born child. Jackson grunted his approval when her husband immediately handed his horse's reins to his brother and headed to the house.

"Looks like our young Martha's getting ready to deliver your next grandbaby, Mama," he whispered in her ear. "Betcha if it's a girl she looks just like you."

Sarah closed her eyes and tilted her head to the sun, her grandchildren's laughter echoing from the barn, the scent of hay and horse, and Jackson, filling her senses.

Though all their children had dark hair and dark eyes thanks to her heritage, she'd always known who their sons' fathers were. While others might not notice, their youngest son favored Nate, while their eldest son held his head at exactly the same angle as Jackson. But she'd never been able to determine who her daughter took after. Not that it made a difference to either Jackson or Nate.

Or her. She loved them all equally. As they loved her.

ABOUT THE AUTHOR

Married to her college sweetheart, and the mother of two sons, and grandmother to three grandsons, Leah Braemel is the only woman in a houseful of men—even their dog and cat are male. She loves escaping the ever-multiplying dust bunnies by opening up her laptop to write about sexy heroes and the women who challenge them.

Sign up for Leah's newsletter by scanning the QR code or visiting her website at LeahBraemel.com.

facebook.com/AuthorLeahBraemel

twitter.com/LeahBraemel

instagram.com/LeahBraemel

bookbub.com/authors/leah-braemel

www.ingramcontent.com/pod-product-compliance
Lightning Source LLC
Chambersburg PA
CBHW021700110726
47902CB00007B/2003